A SERIAL KILLER.

D0631132

SNAPSHOTS FOR

A SERIAL KILLER:

A FICTION AND A PLAY

Robert Peters

GLB Publishers   San Francisco

Published in the United States by
GLB Publishers
P.O. Box 78212, San Francisco, CA 94107 USA

Cover Design by
Black Eagle Productions

Publisher's Cataloging in Publication
(Prepared by Quality Books Inc.)

Peters, Robert.
  Snapshots for a serial killer : a fiction and a play / by Robert
Peters.

  p. cm.
  1-879194-07-4

  1. Prose poems. 2. Murderers--Psychological aspects--Poetry.
3. Murderers--Psychological aspects--Fiction. 4. Gays--California
--Fiction.   I. Title.

PN1059.P76P4 1992   808.81
                           QBI91-1873

First printing, March, 1992
10 9 8 7 6 5 4 3 2 1

BOOKS BY ROBERT PETERS

Poetry

FOURTEEN POEMS
SONGS FOR A SON
THE SOW'S HEAD AND OTHER POEMS
EIGHTEEN POEMS
BYRON EXHUMED
RED MIDNIGHT MOON
CONNECTIONS: In the English Lake District
HOLY COW: Parable Poems
COOL ZEBRAS OF LIGHT
BRONCHIAL TANGLE, HEART SYSTEM
HAWTHORNE
CELEBRITIES: IN MEMORY OF MARGARET DUMONT
THE PICNIC IN THE SNOW: Ludwig II of Bavaria
IKAGNAK: The North Wind
BRUEGHEL'S PIG

Criticism

THE CROWNS OF APOLLO: Swinburne's Principles of
    Literature and Art
PIONEERS OF MODERN POETRY (with George Hitch ❀
THE GREAT AMERICAN POETRY BAKE-OFF: First,
Second, Third, and Fourth Series
THE PETERS BLACK AND BLUE GUIDES TO CURRENT
    LITERARY PERIODICALS:
    First, Second, and Third Series
PETERS VISITS W. S. BURROUGHS (privately printed)
HUNTING THE SNARK: A Compendium of New Poetic
    Terminology

Editions

THE LETTERS OF JOHN ADDINGTON SYMONDS (with
   Herbert Schueller)
AMERICA: JOURNAL OF A VISIT (by Edmund Gosse)
THE POETS NOW SERIES OF LIVING AMERICAN POETS
   Scarecrow Press
LETTERS TO A TUTOR: The Tennyson Family
LETTERS TO H. G. DAKYNS
AUSTRALIAN POETS (the best of *Poetry Australia*. Edited
   with Paul Trachtenberg)

Memoirs

CRUNCHING GRAVEL: On Growing Up in the Thirties
FOR YOU, LILI MARLENE: A Memoir of World War II
A NIGHT WITH THE UNDERTAKER'S GRANDSON: My
   Sister's Story

*Please see the end of this book for
additional titles and availability of
other works by* Robert Peters.

ACKNOWLEDGEMENTS

A special thanks to Paul Trachtenberg, Peter Schneidre, Paul Vangelisti, Jesse Glass Jr., Charles Plymell, and Bill Warner for their suggestions which have influenced the shaping of this book. To Dennis Cooper, who knows more about these matters than almost anyone else, I owe much for advice and inspiration. Thanks to Carl Weissner and the editors of *Warten* (Berlin) for featuring the book in their winter, 1991 issue. To Ron Offen, editor of *Free Lunch*, for careful editorial suggestions for the selections he was first to publish, to Michael Hathaway, editor of *Chiron Review*, to Larry Oberc, to Joan Jobes Smith and the editors of *Pearl* who featured the work, and to the editors of *Vice Versa* and *Onthebus* I am most grateful.

It is not right that everyone should read the pages which follow; only a few will be able to savor this bitter fruit with impunity. Consequently, shrinking soul, turn on your heels and go back before penetrating further into such uncharted, perilous wastelands. Listen well to what I say: turn on your heels and go back, not forward, like the eyes of a son respectfully averted from the august contemplation of his mother's face; or rather like a formation of very meditative cranes, stretching out of sight, whose sensitive bodies flee the chill of winter, when, their wings fully extended, they fly powerfully through silence to a precise point on the horizon, from which suddenly a strange wind blows, precursor of the storm.

  — Lautréamont, *Maldoror*, tr. by Paul Knight

The fascination of murder is itself curious. Murder is not just killing. Murder is a lust to get at the very quick of life itself, and kill it—hence the stealth and the frequent morbid dismemberment of the corpse, the attempt to get at the very quick of the murdered being, to find the quick and to possess it.

  — D. H. Lawrence, "Edgar Allan Poe," *Studies in Classic American Literature.*

A PREFATORY NOTE ON METHOD

The discerning reader will soon be aware of connections between my killer and the notorious serial murderer, Randy Kraft, who is currently on Death Row, San Quentin, having been convicted of the sex murders of sixteen young men and suspected of killing more than sixty. Most of Kraft's victims met their fate in Southern California where Kraft lived, employed as a computer specialist known for his intelligence. I attended numerous sessions of his lengthy trial in Santa Ana, near my home. Kraft never took the stand in his own defense and has, in fact, denied his guilt. He is currently starting through the appeals process.

Many of Kraft's paradoxes intrigued me; first, his attractive manner, almost winsome, during the trial; second, his positive reputation for generosity and caring among family members and close friends; and third, his immersion in gay life, including much bridge-playing and up-scale socializing. All these seemed contrary to the torture-murders of young men, many of them gay, many not. I was present on the day of his sentencing. Eventually I wrote to Kraft, in care of San Quentin, but the letter was returned, marked "Not An Employee".

Shortly the idea for a book based on Kraft "appeared". I knew at the outset that the creation of "my" killer, while it would tangentially touch Kraft, would not be Kraft. I have limited myself to the salient facts as anyone can find them in the newspaper. These, then, are the broad lineaments; the interior life, which is what I am about, is entirely my creation. For that reason, I never mention Kraft's name. No reader, therefore, should confuse these issues. My invention is no more the actual figure (Kraft) stimulating my work than, say, Robert Browning's bishop was in *The Bishop Orders His Tomb in St. Praxed's Church*, or the doomed priest lover and his mistress in *The Ring and the Book*, both protagonists being based on an actual adultery-

v

murder story of the time. Or, reaching even further back, historians would hardly say that Shakespeare's powerful presentation of his monstrous Richard III more than broadly delineates the actual historical figure. John Keats called this penchant for writers to engage the psyches of characters "playing the chameleon."

Much of my writing, of several book-length monologues for an assortment of personas from saints to murderers, has been inspired by Keats' dictum. *Snapshots For A Serial Killer* is meant to provide yet another slant on the omnipresence of violence in our time, a theme I explored earlier in *The Blood Countess*. There, the notorious female serial killer, Elizabeth Bathory, who bathed in the blood of some seven hundred virgins, arraigns her audience, declaring violence "the religion" of the late twentieth century. The morbid difference and even hostility to individual human lives is, I suggest, one of the central mysteries of our times. By leading my readers through a gamut of feelings regarding my killer (for he presents himself as brutal, as vulnerable, and as craving for his audience to like and understand him), I hope to stimulate their thinking about the violence we currently see on the freeways, in shopping malls, fast food restaurants, and dominating the mass media. Beauty and disease, I conclude, have always been intertwined.

A final note: my killer, though something of an artifact in his sense of physical and natural beauty and in his fondness for language, is such a monster that he wears the mask of being gay without earning the right to be gay. While psychiatrists know little about the motifs of serial killers, it seems a given that labeling such monsters gay or straight has nothing to do with reality. Obviously, my protagonist's idea that "killing is a way of finally loving" is entirely perverse.

PART ONE:

SNAPSHOTS FOR A PERSONAL HISTORY

MY OPEN DOOR

Mom bakes apricot cookies. Dad scoops up iron filings from his shop while reminding me that I need a vocation. My Jockey Shorts could use a scrubbing. My door is open. I've got dope, beer, a light, and much terror. Come, blow up my house. Climb down my rain barrel. I'm whetting knives. Restore that plaster head to the shoulders of Michelangelo's David.

CHILDHOOD SNAPSHOTS

1.

A naked child carries a multi-colored xylophone and a cinnamon teddy bear downstairs. He clutches a brown tiger bedspread. Toy mice squeak tunes on toy instruments. See the Howdy Doody poster and the immaculate room. The child rocks on the floor with his head thrown back. His phony opaque eye glasses aim at a stubble-stucco ceiling where a rubber U.S. Marine doll swims attached by wires and pins.

2.

A scrawny-faced boy arouses himself under a desk, jiggles his thighs and squeezes his rind. He asks to be seen. At recess, he stabs smelly fingers at girls and at boys with long hair. "If I had a lantern," he says to his plump friend Rudolph, "I'd guide you through a diddle-sex forest. We'd have fun. I'd pull out your hair. Then I'd fuck you and you could fuck me."

BOY VERBALIST

Always, at night, outside my window, the white azaleas of day, tinged with rust, turn into red amaryllises. I am frightened. Blossoms time-lapsed into enormous sticky petals suck me in to their ravenous enzymes. Goodby, Planet Earth. Will Daddy kiss his little son goodnight? Will he extol me for having won the class prize for reading books this year. As usual, I'm compulsive. Jekyll and Hyde. Far From the Madding Crowd. Catcher in the Rye. Tolkein. I even tackled The Sound and the Fury, getting through it without any help from teacher. "You'll outwit time's cradle," she said. "You have style."

I flesh out stories and poems, most of which I save pasted into old wallpaper sample books. I have the largest vocabulary in my school. Yet I am fragile. I wish I'd been named *Robert Louis*, after Stevenson. From Goodwill, teacher bought me Stevenson's books. I still play with toy cars, firetrucks, and long-haired rubber boy-dolls. I draw hard-ons with ink.

"I have high hopes for you," teacher says, promoting me. Dad reads the sports pages, the TV Guide, and advertising brochures. Yes, he scans for news of assorted Mutual Funds. Since I'm as compulsive about the fridge as I am about reading, my body is pudgy. I handle eating even better than I do books.

In high school, I have fun goofing off, acquiring a taste for walnuts, molasses, and sperm. Merchant marines strolling in Long Beach supplant Stevenson's pirates.

I can never come, it seems, at the right time—I am always left with one hand on my groin, the other on my mouth aching for more. Bitter red-skinned cherries and acrid tangerines deceive me. True, I have one or two friends who whip me off without expecting reciprocity, in the citrus groves. I am "cute." They tremble pulling down

3

my pants, fearing I'll change my mind. During such times, whenever I cross my thighs, intercrural, I hear crickets rubbing their legs, rabbits bouncing through mesquite, cottonwoods dripping silver, each leaf a shred of human skin. Though I say I like girls, I know male bodies best. I have stashed my reading certificates in a cigar box. I no longer scribble in a journal. Every time, it seems, after a few sentences, imaginary lovers assault me. One rips out a page, crushes it into a ball, and flings it into the toilet. Often there is blood and the wail of torture. My beloved fat Granny returns from the dead: "Your meat's raw. Your nerves hiss. Take this knife." Am I crazy? The old woman's snickering face spews viscous green slime, then sinks. Oh, to be loved! I smother my mouth in dahlias, so purple, so like death clad in chiffon and adorned with fabulous pearls.

ORANGE COUNTY SCENE WITH SURFERS, ETC.

This sprawl, place of my birth, my plastic baby rocker, my crib, a mobile of fish jiggling inches from my chubby eyes, my front yard of Bermuda grass and the cement water meter cover, the ornamental plums ubiquitous here, my dainty feet. I soon gave up sucking my thumb for sucking cock. If plant imagery is appropriate (I'm into gardening), I'm an exotic philodendron. Other boys are sycamores and lodgepole pines. I hide everything in orange groves. If you kneel beneath the frost-softened fruit you'll know where I've been.

I see elaters, sow bugs, red ants, cut worms, supermarket parking lots, the neighbor's pit bull, the Presbyterian church, the widowed Mrs. Austin who lost her mate and three sons in a freeway crash. Through Christmas binoculars I spy plovers feeding and bare asses when the surfers drop wet suits. I see the high rise Security Pacific National Bank where we deposit checks. And I still see the park—before they plundered it for condos. You'll find my footprints there, mine and those of the first person other than my mom I ever kissed. We pressed the insides of our lips together, creating an unpleasant suction and banging our teeth. Giggling, we displayed our cocks. Mine, he said, would always be squiggly. "They do get bigger." I described Dad's whopper. "You can hope," he teased. Well, binoculars, microscopes, or the mind's third eye—none of these. I knew what was wrong, and whipped my ears and buttocks.

MEADOW WITH CREATURES

Hawks rebuffed the winds, then plummeted. I fetched toys, fire trucks, erector sets, the naked Gi Joe doll whose plastic ass I kissed and fondled. I lay back in the parched grass, fantasizing boys taking showers. I asked Nancy Quim to the prom. Whether I was popular didn't matter. Who foresaw plagues of condos usurping these fields? Queen Anne's Lace whispered. Fleecy milkweed pods blew. Thistles rang changes on despair. Butterflies flopped and died. Whistling birds overwhelmed the creosote trees. A wood dove slept on my shoulder. A buck in velvet brushed my face with its chilly nose. After-images of full moons and tinted oranges lingered into afternoon. Even in winter the eucalypti were shaggy. Beech, sycamore, and walnut saplings dropped leaves. Citrus groves were fired. On rare days the San Gabriel mountains glazed with snow. Who thought of torture then? Who thrilled to the pulse of a wren as a boy smashed its skull between his fingers? Who thought of wrenched, outrageous death?

MOTHER AND SON

Mom, I'm eight, and lie face down on your bed. Something's wrong. The knuckle of your right thumb (a wren's head) flattens the knot of my distress. I kiss the blood circulating in your fat neck. I don't sleep for hours. You complain that your arm is numb, that my head sweats. Then I sleep. When I awake (you say it's only two a.m.) you're still there. I spread my arms like bat wings, black satin skin, and fly away. Where? Am I better than everybody else? I am no sissy! I will not be teased. Girls pull down their panties. Other boys pay a penny to see the "penny bank show." I never pee in coffee cans. Dad's on another toot. Where shall I go, Mom? A rainbow arches over a river of sperm. Below, a parched desert moils, a sickly purple. I glue my body to yours and sweat and toss and sleep.

SNAPS FROM A *NATIONAL GEOGRAPHIC*

Mom, thirty, stands beneath an oak on a denuded mangy mountain. She flings granite at a yelping red squirrel. He's spoiling our picnic. "Just like a male," she sneers. "I'll impale that bugger's heart." "Won't his blood drip?" I ask; "do let him go." Three black men with penises stuffed into striped gourds stand crane-like, holding spears adorned with shreds of lion-tail, gazing at sacred cattle with enormous dewlaps.

Dad is a foul-mouthed Farley Granger in jodhpurs who cracks his whip, demeaning glistening mahogany natives. The sun scorches Mom's face. She concocts pitchers of lemonade. She's perfect. She never sweats.

A dragonfly on Dad's arm flashes its pencil of a body. Acacia petals adhere to Dad's nipples. He swats bees from his sweat-soaked head.

An indigo cloud grazes the mountain. The night will be frigid.

Mom cautions me: "I love your pa, though, like all men he's dirty. He can't help it. Sniff his sweat, and sniff his piss. I can tell when he's just wiped his bum. Of course, I don't complain." She distresses me. She would never talk like this in California. Rats dash to underground burrows. The hens are cackling.

"But now," Mom says, "look at those new-born kittens. See how they stand, tiny grey hippos with bursting milk-swollen bellies. Be sure the dingoes don't snatch them."

"That's the wrong continent, Mom," I say proudly. "Dingoes live in Australia." She returns to being Deborah Kerr, pure, sexless, and codified. She's drawn nooses around me. "Dirty old pup" is her epithet for Dad.

Through the corrugated partition between our safari space, I hear them fuck. Dad makes all the racket. I hate him. Mom, an orange lily on her back, fears Dad will be offended when she assumes a post-coital white voice, wipes herself, and rearranges her hair.

MOM, ON HER DAY

Something human resides in this rose swathed with fern and ribbon. Mom's not expecting a gift. She's learned, she whines, that the best presents you give yourself, an onanistic view of barter, appreciation, and exchange. To please her is useless. Yet, I love her when she sings Glen Miller tunes and concocts apple pies lavish with buttery sugar crumbs. I try hard to love her, a face of affection, a mouth of mirth glinting with fine teeth.

My guess is she's always hated sex. The music was foul, for there was none. The conjunction of male and female parts was foul. A harsh bone rammed her flower. That's when I was conceived, when the vital part of Dad's load burned along Mom's thigh and sent pallid fishy missionaries up her tubes. One little squiggle rode oarless and rudderless up the Congo implanting itself at last in the uterine throat creating me. If I have misled you, I'm sorry. My tale is bitter-sweet. The grey souls of snails snuffed Mom's wailing.

She accepts the rose—I surprise her in the midst of dishing up pork chops, beets, and mashed potatoes. She wears a sloppy apron. Her gray hair flies out in strands, and she has burned the meat. I hold the flower to her nose. She sighs, puts down the serving dish, and pecks my cheek.

YEARBOOK PHOTO

Kenny Thomas' dad owned the local dry cleaning plant. Kenny was zitless, had no BO, and his nails were perfect. For laughs he rented a hearse for the Junior prom. I followed him everywhere—I don't think he knew. My flattop hair cut aped his. My shoes were wing-tipped. He drank and had his own Ford coupe. He drove fast, he said, so that the trees appeared to be undressing. He hit a eucalyptus near the public library.

During his memorial service at the Congregational Church girls dab their eyes. Gardenias, his favorite flowers, waft from his coffin. His coupe sits in the schoolyard as a *memento mori*.

Later, alone in the park, I tear out my hair. A broken bird eludes the shadow of a boy with a stick.

"COOL HAND LUKE"

With his legs shackled and his hands shackled Luke with a blunt shovel excavates a six foot, shoulder-wide slit in the packed earth adjacent to the frame porch where the overseer sits picking his nose, shucking peanuts, and whistling. "Eat good ole 'merican pie, boy."

Most grave diggers rest until the loam they've overturned loses its sheen and earthworms have sucked themselves back below the riotous, moist, quack-grass roots.

"Get workin', boy. You's only half-way done. An' keep your hot white tits off that cool bank. You ain't gittin' no respite here, you son of a bitch. Dig! Dig!"

Road-gang mates toss down wild asters, thistles, and morning glory vines. They throw him a plaid shirt.

"Now, boy, lie supine. We don't want your eyes accusin' us. Yours is the crime. A perfect fit."

The prisoners grab picks and shovels. Those refusing are whipped. They cut out his tongue. He was so young. They'll not keep any of his clothes, or brag, or confuse the red tremor of the sand with any larger purpose.

FAMILY PORTRAIT

The Judds down the block lived on olives, lemons, and pickles. The front yard was smothered in cuke vines. "Dildoes," we joked. When senility struck the old folks we assumed that vinegar pickled their brains. They were hostile. I could smell the wife inside the house. The two daughters dropped out of school and sewed gowns for the yacht club set. Their scissors and treadles clattered. When they jabbed themselves, stiletto pain flew up the chimney and over the cuke vines. The son, Rick, would show me his cock, boasting that it was full of piss and vinegar. He used Clearasil and became a San Francisco poet. I'm sure he's gay; he smells of balsam branches. When he ate with me, I dissuaded him from carrying on, for his leather jacket snowed dandruff. He drank wine and went home to his folks. Now, tonight, I'm so lonely I feel crazy. If he were still here, I'd scarf up his dandruff, savoring it on my tongue, rolling it into a ball.

COW GIVING BIRTH

My favorite of Grandpa's cows was a small blonde hornless creature with a perfect white forehead star. She usually avoided the filthy ditches and the marl and dung-infested corners of the corral. "Lady," pale in moonlight, reminded me of Mom. Obsessed, up to my knees in warm swamp muck, I followed her to where she feasted on water lilies.

I knew when she was pregnant. Her sides, swollen, carried a cask of wine. Her udder every day swelled. I curried her and sprayed her with Fly-Tox to dissuade horse flies from depositing eggs in her hide. I would express them, suety and squirming, with my thumbs.

One afternoon Lady hunched and lowed. Her pained mouth curved up higher than her shoulders. Her teeth dripped saliva and clover juice. I encircled her neck with my arms. When she shook her head I backed off. Strings of matter dripped, purplish, iridescent, almost balloon-like in their sheen. She moaned. An odor of zinc fell from the sky. Sweat fell. I grabbed up a twig and beat my legs. The calf's muzzle was visible. The body was an exotic blood-flower. The whole calf, umbilicus attached, dropped. Lady turned, licking, nudging, until the calf stood with its legs at crazy angles. Granny came with a pitchfork, and when the placenta, as large as a washtub and radiant with viscous pink, orange, and purple eyes, dropped, she speared it to prevent Lady's eating it, thereby fouling her milk.

BOY KILLING A HEN

Mom had planned chicken and dumplings for Easter Sunday dinner. Yes, there was the sterile hen she'd marked, a scraggly white mess whose rear was smeared with dung as thick as cardboard. Her floppy comb was pallid, her tiny ears oyster white. At 5 a.m. I crept from bed, pulled on my overalls, took a shortcut through the cabbage patch to the hen yard where, drawn by the morning sun, the fowl were emerging, hoping for oats and cracked corn. A blue mist filled the draw between the birch woods leading to the lake a mile away. Squash flowers climbed the coop wire screen.

At the chopping block, a chunk of white pine turned on end, I grabbed a hatchet and stared into the face of a gentian. It grimaced, saying "no," for the wind had risen. Propping the hatchet against the chopping block, I cornered the hen. She squawked and struggled, then calmed when I thrust down her bedraggled wings, clapping them tight to her shanks. She gasped for air.

The interior of her mouth resembled a cotton swab used for wiping a wound. Her tongue was a red awn of wheat. Her death would be clean, and, since it would be swift, lovely. She ruffled her feathers and jerked. Once on the chopping block, she stretched her neck, and her head slipped easily into the groove. Her leached eyelids opened and closed revealing phlegm. The raised axe fell, striking her brain pan, leaving half of a skull behind. Angry blood arced over wood chips, thistles, and pig weed. She died in my hands, for I would not let her slam her stunned body about, rearing her headless hard neck in crazy parody of what she'd been. Her electric blood, like a death angel's, roared through me.

WOMAN WITH RABBIT

I hoped the woman who bred rabbits would give me one. My favorite, jet black, was unable to hop within the confines of his horrid wire cage. A white doe with black markings shared the hutch. They're "making bunnies," the woman said, adding that "minks fuck more but don't have litters as big."

When I brought Bermuda grass to the mesh the big buck munched, dropping saliva on my fingers. He'd even interrupted a shuddering copulation. The lips of death and sex are thin.

When I asked for the buck, the woman fingered a rusty safety pin holding her apron to her blouse. "Your grandma won't like it," she said, her eyes like cold zinc. "Please? I'll pay for him." "No way, Jose. Summer's nearly done and you'll go to California to school."

I gazed between her beefy brows, at her third eye, at a declivity waiting to be smacked with her blunt hatchet. A pomegranate shed seeds through me. "It would serve her right," rang a voice from a cistern, as in a Sunday School text.

The buck, the woman explained, had sired so many offspring he was now screwing his "kids." She, the woman, would not risk letting the strain peter out. "What applies to humans applies to bunnies." She grabbed the animal, yanking him forth. "He'll dress out from six to seven pounds," she declared, "which is exactly what the customer ordered."

"Let me hold him," I said.

"Well, only if you clamp him tight. If he gets away, a fox will eat him."

I glimpsed her black wooly armpit hair. I caught the gamey odor of the stocking cap pulled over her ears. Her gingham dress was so tight the crack of her ass was visible.

Her knees were knobs of suet; even behind the knees were globs of blue-veined fat. Her work shoes seemed of heavy slate secured with scraps of rawhide. I reached for the hatchet. "What you doin' with that thing, boy?"

She banged the buck's head on a plank supporting his cage. "Instant death," she said. His brain shattered into a host of crabs squirming for shelter. The woman's eyes were the ends of silver screws. I wanted to shove poisoned grapes down her gullet. I wished I'd not dropped the hatchet.

She strung the animal to a nail, slit its throat, and hacked off its head. She next made an incision around each of its legs, near the feet, so that all she had to do was give one jerk and the fur detached itself. This she did with the ease she'd have used in stripping one of her six kids of a snowsuit.

Without saying goodby, I crossed the road to my grandparents' house. Behind me, the buck's black fur looked glazed. A pair of blackbirds struggled over the guts. It was the same in California. Death was a ghost with a beard, long eyelashes, and hair down to his waist. He wore a nightgown and held a sheep crook. Hosts of bleeding children, rabbits, squirrels, quail, and deer scattered before Him. I felt lashes across my back. Gladioli whipped my mouth. I was stumbling over myself. I was not yet able to fly.

SNAPSHOT OF GOD WITH SINNER

Night tolls bells. Hairless camels sleep against one another. Their rat pink cold skins. Ugh! Tomorrow I'll eat raw pork. Don't tell me about the next day or the next. "Biplanes are crammed with strawberries," you say. That's weird! "Rotisseries turn sizzling microscopic suet globules of DNA on spits," you exclaim. That's crazier. God's slobbering in a corner. He shows me my path. He holds a cerecloth. He lops off the heads of newts. He counts frigid sparrows. He counts my crotch hairs as they fall.

SAFE FOR THE NIGHT

The patio door rattles as you enter with an armful of blue delphiniums. There's a red steak in your blond hair, as though you had brushed against the rusty iron scrollwork supporting the patio roof. You are winsome. You know I've craved you as I might a fringe of expensive lace or a wrist full of ocean surf suitable for swallowing. I strip you, admiring the interplay of blue tones against the milk. There's an amaryllis at your groin with an erect stamen gilt with pollen. A pearl, moist, wets my finger. I taste it, find it faintly carbolic with a hint of crushed leek. My lips are smeared. Silence whishes. Frost shakes the pepper tree. Safe for the night.

YOU NEED ME

I'm a parenthesis ( ) circumscribed, though only partially since I may escape through either top or bottom. I slither in when the drapes are drawn, as a fat, exotic, multicolored, spiny caterpillar, writhing over your pastel sheets, as a death-worm obsessed with its mouth, its tail, its blatant sex, depositing slime, flatulent, creeping to your throat as you sleep wound in pain, misery, and hate. You want things better, a surfer savior with chocolate and KY on his hands and a purple whip inherited from a chastising father. You want Marilyn Monroe, James Dean, and Elvis to return. No more screened images without stops, merged in flash. "At least," you plead, "keep the junk mail coming, for each piece was touched by a human hand."

Everyone lies: the whines of a man who's savaged his daughter. Whines of a wife tightening throat wires, flattening her breasts, sealing her cunt with axle grease. Whines of a teenage son kissing a boy, who is doomed to chew stolen jock straps and flog his meat while licking his teeth until his tongue bleeds. Paraphiliac. The fox snaps the gingerbread man. The executioner, cobra-hooded, with fangs like spikes filed into hard-penny nails, infects you with AIDS. I know your pain. You can't live without me.

PART TWO:

SNAPSHOTS FOR MURDER

RED BOUGAINVILLEA

I should feel more. I'll try again to say I love you, though I may not mean it. A stench of mushrooms. No, they're phallic knobs spewing backyard poisons where entwined we ejaculated near the blue hydrangeas. Massive backyard nasturtiums flap their tongues. Johnny-jump-ups riot with joy. A Lavish bougainvillea. I crave rotting leaves, and the streaming red flesh of plums. I've shattered you. Your head is in a gas station dumpster, your arms—I've forgotten where I threw them, your torso is impaled on a spike. I should feel more than I do.

MOUNTAINSCAPE WITH ACID

We are spread-eagle on a midnight couch of ice fallen from a purple sky stained for our pleasure with Northern Lights. Ice-asters spring from my eyes. Frozen rose petals trickle from my lips. We are in a golden vestibule.

You had stumbled even before the acid flashed through your brain's neuron crystals pulsing with salmon and teal. We were at the frozen lake—at the narrow end, the one shaped like a goat's udder, which was solid. The ponderosas were flailing, so it seemed, warning us against thin ice. You were suddenly my child and I wiped snot from your nose. Though you giggled I knew you hurt. I was only old enough (you were ten years younger) to absorb at most a flick of your anguish. You pushed that booming garbage can, broke off your stiletto heels, and sent them soaring. Though we were under a brilliant moon (I could have sung a rhapsody on John Dillinger's cock), I lost the trajectory. I now believe that those heels were slivers of hate inside your eyes pretending to be kisses. I wanted to protect you as you slam dunked the cans, the ice-palace floor crazed with images of insane floppy ears out to testify against us; we were queers lost on a mountain. Laughing, we flew towards the brink of the drink. I followed, as in a dream of snarling tubas and blaring cornets. I knew you did not want to die, so screamed like a peacock as the corrugated cans (you were swirling two of them now) reverberated like aluminum bones clanging over bloody water. Joy died on your lips. We returned to the shelter of the massive roots eroded by the ebb and fall of the tarn where we had dropped our thermal jackets. "I feel lecherous," you said. "Let's fuck." You yanked at my pants. "Let's do it standing up," I said. "Let's really make this ice boom. Piss on me first." "Mother Truth," you jibed, imitating Charles Boyer in the Casbah. The ponderosas shivered. Our bodies were like plump ground squirrels. We could have sated ourselves on sky milk. Then, a sudden breeze spilled coded messages. I have always held too many opinions.

First I was your parent, then your child, then a frozen ear craving to listen to all you'd say, disturbing me. I'd hoped to sound wise, no longer "mysterious," as you said, "and capable of malice, even of mayhem." I could not sleep. The wide couch of the snow-drift forest floor invited us as the LSD crazed our brains. There was a vivid blare of blue. Who knew (and we were ready for this) if we would slowly numb to ice, to be found by handsome forest rangers, hand in hand, with blistered smiles on our lips. Later, dawn floated in, crackling into pink light, illuminating the mountains. There was a moth on your cheek.

MARRIED COUPLE

Yes, as you must surmise, I am apprehensive about just how much Jim, my erstwhile lover/room-mate knows of my life. He travels for an aerospace corporation. His sexual ardor has cooled. He brags to other gays of our "open marriage," which means we can trick with strangers. After all, most of my pick-ups leave alive. We have occasional "three ways."

To tell Jim the truth would be like smashing him with a club. For Jim's harmonious and a bit masochistic, so prefers the passive role. He loves having his scrotum nipped and his nipples snapped with battery starter clamps. He has never, as I have, found homosexuals disgusting.

To be accurate, we both love the inception of pleasure, a jazz piano, English boy sopranos, alyssum, and the mad-wort of death. I prefer the Rolling Stones to the Beatles. With Jim, it's the other way around. We love Country Western music. Yes, Loretta Lynn and Randy Travis. At one point, to please Jim I learned bridge. Jim liked playing the boards. As a treat I'd bake lasagna. Once I used ground buffalo meat. The guests, despite the cheese and garlic, found it "strong." Eating buffalo, Jim laughed, hastened the death of the old West.

DYING LEFT ARM

Summer. 4 p.m. I lie beside you with my left hand, palm down, beneath your head. I'd hoped to sleep this way, to join you; but my blood, crystallized by your weight, threatens to shatter my arm. In the darkened room, your throat pulses. The tail light of a yacht far off at sea grows dim. I thrust my free arm to the floor, to the varnished, cool planks. An egret ruffled by fear beats its wing against the patio glass, mistaking the surface for the safe ocean marsh. Still, I do not move. My left arm is dying. You are killing it. In this dream there is terror, for you can't garrote me though I am immobilized. Tell me about it tomorrow, or later this evening when we go for coffee and pizza, and you wear your black suit, the one speckled with dandruff and blood. I hate knowing the time. I'm angry, blaming you.

MAD WOMAN IN A SWING

If she were to stop swinging, the tree trimmers, beefy Chicanos aloft in their bucket lifts near the Rogers Senior Citizen Center, would cease chopping palm fronds. Do the fecund, fallen branches, loaded with maturing dates, stun her? How can I tell? I'd hoped for a calm morning walk.

I won't be her friend or toss pebbles at ground squirrels nibbling the dates for their alcohol.

"No, No, No," she keeps shouting as she pumps the kiddies' swing, neither intensifying or slowing her speed. She's in her mid-twenties, black-haired, chubby, wearing jeans and one of those bandanna halters which bares a lower fold of breast. Her hair falls from her head like strands of rope. One of her hands grasps the swing, the other holds a letter to her face. The news is obviously scarlet, for her bitter shouts fail to cool the paper. She's incredulous, sobbing, brutalized.

Moving in, I pelt her with dates. She never stops reading the letter. She never looks up.

I'd like to think I could have held her—after twisting the swing, slowing it. But comforting the living who survive the dead is impossible. You can't comfort the dead. Days later, I am sickened by her green howls.

ROSAMUND SEEN IN
COMPROMISING POSITIONS

"I'm very angry," she laughed, jamming her hand, palm down, in a pool of slime on the chrome dinette table. I thought she'd spit out her teeth. Her curled hair which was so lovely before she served the veal chops with their little Easter sleeves of butcher paper was now a mass of hissing snakes. "I hate life, and I think I hate you." She sent her hand for her hairbrush. The dime store engagement ring, which I had placed on her finger in jest, winked at our failure. She threw the ring in my face.

Thinking about this now makes me vomit. And I have not been drinking. Nor am I stoned. For a week, during our experiment in "living together" we'd held one another, demanding no more than that the quilts be snug under our chins. "You will," she said, "let my cat out at night." We would cross the lurid sex line only if no fat lips sucked us in. "I am not your death's head moth," I said. Moreover, when I'd necked other women I never touched their nether parts. My erotic cards always collapsed before I reached those Tierra del Fuegos. I could not bring myself to tell Ros this, up front. "If you want to play house, etcetera," I said.

At the office she wore svelte, mannish suits and maneuvered agendas over the shoals. She was divorced. She began lingering near my computer, occasionally resting her red nails on the back of my neck. Her chin resembled William Holden's in "Golden Boy." I wanted her to rape me, acting the male who designs both the plot and the denouement: the one who wipes your cock of excess semen.

To confess, I've always desired that sex be done *to* me, by either male or female. Which does matter. I never reciprocate fully. Despite what I've just said, I prefer to dominate, and, I tell you that flesh is flesh. Yet, I've always been more comfortable with men. What you know, i.e.,

33

your own body won't fail you when mirrored in another body of the same sex.

Well, back to Ros: nothing happened on Saturday or Sunday. On Monday she stripped, buzzed in my ear, then stripped me. The evening news had just come on. "I think about sex all the time," she declared, grasping my shaft. "You don't seem to..." "What?" "Think about sex all the time."

I had always masturbated over breasts. "Jugs" (as we called them) smothered my face, leaving little channel openings for my breath. Oh, I loved to nuzzle! Nuzzling Ros's breasts was fun. They resembled oval lozenges, not the archetypal balloons of smutty jokes. With a nipple cradled in each hand I had the absurd image of preparing to speak via intercontinental telephone. A strand of flesh led from her nipple to her chest, etc. I wanted to reach Prince Charles of England and say I craved to suck his ears.

We rolled together off the bed. She wet her fingers with saliva and retracted my foreskin. Her buttocks were hairless, and I was pleased, for hairy cracks always look best on men. When I cupped a buttock, it quivered: a consciousness neither liquid nor solid touched with a tinge of flame. I'd give it a try.

She smoothed my hand along her labia, which I did not mind, since we were French kissing. She tried to insert my penis, riding me and quivering. A lizard scuttled over my chest. She held me so tight I couldn't withdraw. She bit my throat. She rattled, and when she came, I faked an orgasm, one true to the Easter picture of Savior and Lamb graced with a Palm Sunday leaf. When she realized I would not stay, she opened the door.

34

AUNT VIDA

After Aunt Vida's funeral, the relatives gather in her only son's Beverly Hills apartment. Danny is a slick, black-haired, obese trader in women's undergarments imported from Korea. He smuggles opium among the garter belts. He has a jacuzzi, which he insists we see, pointing to a pile of swim apparel (all new, of course) for those of us who wish to soak our bereavement in the swirling pool. He likes jade lamps shaped like Buddhas and genuflecting elephants. Images of pheasants and peacocks on plaques of beaten copper hang above pastel decorator couches. Plate glass coffee tables stand on gold griffin legs. "Good to see you, cousin," he says. "You should visit more often. I've got some great Hong Kong pussy flicks. Wanna watch a few, after the family thins out?"

The oldsters, including the aunt's uremic husband Ed, quack a few times and fall asleep in soft chairs. When Uncle Ed bubbles, his lips flop. Everywhere there's a white smell of funeral gladioli. Relatives shuffle and squawk, bobbing their duck and duckling heads near tables laden with funeral meats and sweets. Danny's china, plain, has a tasteful gold border. Linen napkins. Modernistic silver knives, forks, and spoons. Nephews and nieces in party garb toss cake, cheese, and pie into the pool. They set gaggles of inflated plastic ducks sailing from one end to the other.

I don't know why I'm here, for Aunt Vida, dear soul, was for me an old sepia print. Like most men in my family, Uncle Ed was manipulated by wife and daughter. Sure, I'm sorry she's dead, although for the past month she spent her days watching TV from a wheelchair, farting and dribbling at the mouth. She once gave me some wool socks. She despised her parents who lived on a farm, my Wisconsin Gram and Gramps.

"I'm into computers," I say as my glance wanders off to

a long-legged, big-shouldered adolescent cousin.

"Oh," Cousin Danny says, cramming his mouth with ham and a fat roll of red cheese. "Do you like the music?" Danny asks. It was Montovani. "A bit old-fashioned. But the older folks enjoy it."

"I've never been much for family gatherings," I declare. I might just as well have said: "Your cats are sodomizing one another by the pool." For he is not listening. His eyes are replete with dollar signs. If I cranked his ear his pupils would come up lemons.

"I have to go," I say. "A nice funeral, don't you think?" He extends a fat hand. "Mom would have been pleased, although the hair-dresser did over-crimp her curls. She always liked her scalp to breathe, wanted her hair loose." He shrugged his shoulders. "You can't have everything? Now she's in the ground, who'll care?" "Do you think she'll go to Heaven bald?" I ask. "She'd lost all her hair, right?" He laughs. "That's sick, cousin, very sick."

I hurry to my car, pop in Jagger's "Flowers," and race home. There's rain. Small glossy puddles glisten in the street. I have a crazy image of Aunt Vida as a baked pumpkin swathed in fluffs of white dacron. Her swollen lips are purple. Her throat has been slashed.

HEROIC DEATHS WITH FLOWERS
After passages in Homer and Virgil

Weighed down by his helmet, Gorgythion's head dropped to one side, like the lolling head of a garden poppy, heavy with seed and the showers of spring.

Euryalus, friend of Nisus, tumbled into death. The blood flowed down his handsome limbs. His neck, collapsing, reclined on his shoulder: even as a purple flower, severed by the plow, falls slack in death, or poppies, as with weary necks, bow their heads weighted down by sudden rain.

For Hyacinthus, the wound was past all cure. So, in a garden, if one breaks off a violet or poppy or lilies, bristling with their yellow stamens, and they droop over and cannot raise their heads, but look on earth, so sank the dying features of Apollo's friend. The neck, its strength all gone, lolled on the shoulder.

JOURNAL ENTRIES

I scribble in my journal, the maroon leather one I began with a prayer to Jesus. I'm hoping that He'll turn the pages, keeping the score in a run of B-Flat Minor arpeggios, execution eighth and sixteenth notes.

You stand there with your legs apart, in the dark, railing. *Monster?* Is the word triplicate chocolate on your palate?

My good intentions have been mocked by persons scarier than you. Despite your vicious gossip, I am normal. You think I don't see you, for the table lamp sheds its glow over my hairy arms and the pen I hold. Look, the paper I write on is unlined. That should tell you something of my steady nerves. Imagine that I'm Columbus, or Jack the Ripper, or an Inquisitioner grasping an ice-white axe.

What shall I write? "Canadian geese fly to the moon? Disneyland Independence Day parades have begun? A green monkey is actually orange?" My right nut matches yours? My eyes burn. Perhaps they have seen too much. Come in. Flash for me. Whisper obscenities over my shoulder. Extinguish the lamp. Kiss me.

NEPHEW DOING HIS HOME WORK

"I love you, Uncle," says Tim, bringing a white hand to my wrist. My sister's grandfather clock bangs. A cat hisses. The kitchen table is round. "I love you, too, Tim." He returns to his math. "Will I ever get this stuff? If you weren't helping, I'd flunk." I laugh. "It's not really that bad, is it?" He's wearing surfer baggies. A small fig is visible between his legs. "The next problem, Tim?"

Tim's ready to cry. The problem is on the speed of a ball and its arrival in a catcher's mitt. "OK, Tim," I say. "Just take charge. You're not dumb. It's only a silly riddle. "What does it have to do with throwing a ball? I'm good at that." He scrawls a diagram in his notebook. "Work from what you know," I say, "then we'll fill in the blanks."

I wait, imagining brown-skinned seeds in a split pear. The dribble of honeyed plum sweat from a fractured bole. Who will care for Tim? A knuckle raps the table. I love the vulnerable dip at the back of his neck, below the hairline, where the tendons create a rift. I touch the spot. "You're doing fine," I say. "I've got it!" he exclaims. "I've solved it."

DISNEYLAND

An angel with a red devil's face, wearing a white Botti-cellian dress with gossamer wings attached, hovers over the zinnias planted in designer plots around the clock tower near the railroad station and the central esplanade. Security men in blue blazers scrutinize the guests. I scurry into a toilet, take a leak, and when I return there's no angel. I say nothing to Jim who is with me. He has found his own apartment. I knew the split was coming. "Your life-style has changed," he says in the jargon of the day, little knowing how right he is. "You won't miss me. You can keep the Persian rug, and I'll take half of the house plants." I agree to pay for his interest in the TV and the stereo.

Half way up Main Street, if you look over to the left, the sidewalk slopes a little. Perhaps the Andreas fault buckled it. You can tell it best if you line up the asses of two lithe men of a similar height; you'll see how one, just for a moment, stands above the other. Those inches are important to me, for minutiae clue us in.

Though Disneyland isn't perfect, it's a great place if you are compulsively neat. You'll never find a dead opossum or rat here. Old people with heart attacks are immediately shuffled off. In "Pirates of the Caribbean" violence and mayhem are "sicklied o'er," as the poet says, with fairy tale compote. When an angel flaps his wings in order to be airborne again, you'll hear a plop as though a merganser hit the ground. Happy Sandman strokes your eyes. The boys who collect debris in plastic dustpans are cute and passive. Bearded gents are green kids again. Old women menstruate. No one slams you down.

And here comes the parade! Aromatic good cheer wafts from the glossy brass and silver horns of the band. Nary a cloud traverses the sky above the butterscotch hills. Nary a whiff of smog. Guests are snapping pictures. No planes winging to John Wayne airport disturb the serenity.

On the Jungle Cruise, a guide tells faggot jokes as we approach some black tote-bearers sent up a tree by a pronged rhino anxious to ram their butts. That script writer sure didn't understand sodomy. I want to cry. Brushing sweat from my upper lip (didn't I shave well?), I edge close to a blonde youth in cords speaking German to a blonde girl. I see the head of his cock and touch my knee to his, pretending it's an accident. He returns the pressure, smiles, then moves closer to his date. I begin to shake, then stand. The guide admonishes me to sit. "You were raw meat back there," Jim says. "Yes, what happened? I wanted to take a swim."

At home, I shower. "Don't plan on me for dinner," I say. "I'll dine with the leopards." "I'll be busy packing," Jim says, not hearing me. "I'll probably be gone before you get home." He pauses. "Oh, your sister phoned; she needs your advice."

MYSTICAL FIGURES ON A SCRIM

1.

Purple, rain-soaked dahlias hang like limp rags. Lettuce plants are seeding. Venus, the evening star, swims behind a cloud. Dreary toads *harrumph*. A white rabbit (someone's pet, I'm sure) nibbles Bermuda grass. He nips my finger. A hare's soft lip, a cleft life, zinc-tinctured odor of cinnamon. Phosphorus engulfs my nostrils.

2.

Dead, he flies towards golden filigrees of light where nothing hurts, where souls snap and crackle.

His lips will never again kiss fire. His dead eyes will miss subtle mountain dawns.

STONED YOUTH

Yes, my Mustang's a great car. My leather jacket is great. My stash of pills is great. Your haircut is great. But you've muddied your great boots. There's a great wooden pail of piss, kum, and blood. We'll rev north past all the sleeping condos and oil wells. What great brown fingers you have. You're drunk. Sure, that's a gay bar. I'd say you were straight. We'll leave it at that. "To each his own," as Bette Davis, or was it Gene Tierney, said. I'd like to feel your cock. Pop open the glove compartment. They're all free, Tom. *Tom*, right? From Iowa? Pop six or more. Flex a muscle. Show me some arm. I'm the farmer's daughter. Do you like eating cunt? The nipples of your raspberry tits are hard cherry pits. Tip back your seat. Murmur. The horny wicked witch of the west? Keep slurring your words. There's spit on your chin. There's spit in your eye. A bed behind a rest stop privy, in eucalyptus leaves. Sleep. Sleep. You're mine. You're anonymous. You're anyone I please. Be Ted, be Chris, be Ben, be Randy.

LOVE POEM FOR
A BOY OF THE EVENING

Even more ridiculous than your mutilated ass are the enormous, livid fungi-buttocks of those apes (mandrills?) in the zoo who blast diarrhetic shit over human visitors. Who said this would be sexy? The denuded palms in the ape house reek, crammed with mangy ape souls exploding everywhere as harp strings tinkling, rattling kitchen lids, zithers strummed by angels. You loved, you say, to watch the pot-bellied creatures masturbate their red stringy penises capped with those little absurd mushrooms. The males, you laugh, are exact replicas of old comedian Joe E. Brown. I don't smash your face in because I love blue, even on mandril asses. I do, though, prefer salmon, of the sort that stains beach sunsets. I'll have them both, please, salmon and blue. You know what I mean? I'll play "monkey" if I must. You, then, ride that flatulent truck tire suspended from the leafless cement ape tree, over the ape pool with its rancid mix of feces, urine, and sperm. If you can't oblige, say that the tire rim chafes your skin and we'll move to a pair of sycamores in the aviary. We climb to the upper canopy, free of the lice and other creepy insects dropped by infested parrots and mynah birds. Up there we groom ourselves, wiggle our lurid fungi asses in one another's face, fuck, and scream at the sun (and the moon). They send up water and food via pulley and sponge. Who knows, we may come to love vinegar and gall. This is a love poem for you, boy of the evening.

BODY UNDER THE ICE

In the morning I knew there had been a struggle, for the couch was torn up, the coffee table upended, and there, lying against the tropical fish tank, were the boot laces I had used to strangle him. I felt drowsy, rearranged the couch pillows, and lay back troubled. My lips had numbed, I remembered, as I tried to revive him. Feeling nothing but snow, I set off for the mountains. There, with his body in my arms, I trudged to a small lake covered with magenta ice. Despite posted warnings, I walked out. The ice shivered like a knife slashing silk. I could have fallen through. The body slid forth only half submerged among the startled fishes. Shocked by the frigid water the boy's lungs inflated. His ears were blue. I grabbed a fallen elm branch, struck off some leaves, and pushed on his buttocks. He sank. Puffs of steam rose. The wretched face pressed to the green ice with its lips ajar. I fled. No one had seen. No one would care.

KEEPSAKES

I've always slept well. Pear blossoms drift past my lips. Shadows brush my eyes. Velvet seeps from my pupils, beautiful. A timid housefly hones its forelegs of stickum and tips its furry eyes towards a cobweb in the midst of which waits a fat spider with a silver diamond on its back, pulsating, digesting a white moth. This is life as it is. The house is quiet. My house has treasures where fear sleeps. The spaniel has stopped flopping its leg on the ceramic Italian tile of the kitchen floor. Angel fish in the aquarium sleep while whirling their fins. It's too early for the paper boy. I throw off the blankets and dream that I am on a killing field gathering up objects belonging to my victims. Where each one fell stands a wooden cross, the easier to match my discoveries with the appropriate man, in case I've forgotten. I find a Swiss Army knife, a lock of hair inserted in a glass keepsake, a child's milk tooth. I stash these in my lowest dresser drawer, installing the dead in my house. I've quite a collection of socks, underwear, neckties, shoe laces, and T-shirts from Grand Rapids, Michigan and Salem, Oregon. These objects lack mystical overtones. They are like sea shell collections or bullet casings retrieved from a firing range, as a hobby. On occasion, I have grabbed a pair of jockey shorts or a sock, and, closing my eyes, have clenched it in my fist, rendering the odor of its owner. See me, if you wish, as a rose and the kept object the chaffer chomping inside the rose. All keepsakes are coals in a grate; they may seem nothing but cold ash; but if you strike them, or if they are disturbed and tumble to the fireplace floor, they gash, releasing sparks. I am comfortable then. My heart sleeps. Fear itself, like a peon in a huge sombrero and heavy serape, feels blest by the moon, that icy metal disk. I'll do nothing more tonight. I shall sleep.

YOUTH WITH PEACH

You were easing into manhood. Your family assumed you had died in a large city killed by a panther with a purple tongue, incisors, and huge gonads, who with cash enticed you to his lair. You'll never be a stock broker, write stories, perm, marry, pull teeth, design tennis garb, or sign contracts. You will never see your family again. You came to me.   I was a red-skinned, sunburned peach with a diamond at my core anxious to chisel your teeth. Or, I was a Venus fly-trap clapping shut over you. Yes, what we did! You could barely scribble your name. You hoped to be discovered by a movie mogul, as a sensation. Your right side was your best, and you'd sleep with anybody. I thought your left side best, for that's how I finally positioned you. When I saw your pale flesh redden, I fancied crimson peaches. Your body was sweet. I should know, I drank you. I loved and hated you.

SNAPSHOTS SNAPPED
OF A THEATRE BENEFIT

I greet the octogenarian owner of the palatial home. For almost thirty years, this former actress, an Hungarian, so tan that her eyes glitter like amethysts, has assembled, cajoled, and encouraged local actors and playwrights. Her bare arms are like maroon bratwurst in slim casings glistening with lotion. Purple liver spots. Puckered skin. Turquoise Navajo bracelets, three per arm, adorn her wrists. Her gown, cut from tapestry riotous with roses and vines in the William Morris style, hugs her flat chest in a low rectangular pattern accenting the horny bumps of her cartilaginous upper collar bones; the flesh is a deep freckled amber. Her straight, flaxen hair, tinged with orange, in page-boy style, resembles a cloche hat and boasts a single red rose. Her lips, painted carmine, look crammed with geriatric blood. There are hints of raspberry where her lips meet. Her front teeth are stained. An elegant Peruvian shawl drapes her shoulders. Her long walks and daily swims, winter or summer, in rough Pacific surf, are legendary. She produces elaborate dishes of paprika chicken and veal smothered in onions. She loves hugging people and stroking their faces as if they were lambs. She crams her sentences with information, good feeling, and wit. She assumes that I write plays. "I support the arts," I say. She nods, holds my wrist, and looks past my shoulder to the next person ascending the steps. I don't let her go. She swings her right arm forwards and back as though retrieving a lost oar. "Life is cruel." She gazes straight through me. "You might relish tree resin, or a nubile woman emerging from the surf on a nautilus shell. You do like women, don't you? You can't be too sure these days. I've lived in Europe, you know, where armies like vicious beetles crush civilians in their pincers. My family endured horrors." She loses herself. "Think of me as a night blooming Cereus shrouding your heart." She laughs. "There's something scary about you, a green tinge to your lips. I don't know quite what it is."

VIVISECTION TABLEAU

1.

A famous Victorian surgeon confessed in his journal that he despised ether. He loved screams, the more stentorian the better. During raucous, orgasmic surgeries he'd stop to change his skivvies. This "penchant" he deemed "abominable." Wasn't he saving money for the hospital?

2.

My surfer's screams scale from a basso profundo to an o'erleaping, lovely soprano: a chilling rabid continuo. Iced calf liver with dollops of cream. Raspberries pureed with sperm. The boy's threshing legs, his rock-hard ass, the loins, the agitated hands secured with a belt behind his scarred back. Death's throttle is a blue rush.

3.

John Doe, a Marine, was hitchhiking to Mendocino. I knew he was a faggot. "You made the pass," I said. "You grabbed my crotch before I grabbed yours." "I was drunk," he replied, "and stoned." I hate guys who hide. I photographed him sucking me off. When he was comatose, I plunged scissors into his back and propped him on my gray couch. More snapshots of his uncut, limp cock. As I chopped it off, plus his balls, moans modulated a scale of screams. I turned up the stereo: "Paint it Black."

It's very easy: slice the cartilage cushioning the large upper vertebra. Sever a leg. Sniff the air between the joints. Later, toss the parts from your car. I'm a hero sowing dragon's teeth: His head's on Anaheim Boulevard. His arms are on Terminal Island Freeway. His left leg's behind Broom Hilda's Leather Bar where I dispense drinks. My outfit's hot. My ass is framed by hot black leather casings. I'm Bishop, Acolyte, Master, and Slave. I'm on puma feet, with one hand at my groin, the other jingling a fat ring of keys.

SNAPSHOTS OF ATTACK AND LOATHING

1.

On the honeyed floor of the bar nude males, flower petals tended by leather men, sleep. Railroad spikes arranged on a bed of shaved ice.

Though I always feel less than I am, I crave the pursuit. That's the game. I have my wrist stamped. Sex baboons with livid ass plates shaped like fungi lurk. I posture within a grove of technicolor faces: Mae West, Marlon Brando, James Dean, Marlene Dietrich, Mel Gibson, Liz Taylor, and Marilyn Monroe. I sing along, though I shiver. My nose and tail, like Pinocchio's, blue, are out of joint. Someone's finger jiggles the fluted puckers of my ass hole.

I avoid eye contact and assume a steely gaze. I guzzle Bud straight from the bottle, and flatten my gut beneath my plaid Western shirt.

2.

During adolescence, at the library, if a stranger stroked his crotch I feigned disgust, later suffering bad dreams. If a man in cut-offs sat nearby on a park bench, I snapped my book shut, threw my half-eaten sandwich to the squirrels, and left. If a "queer" walked his setter on a leash, I hurried to the other side of the street. Dad mocked "faggots." So did my classmates even as they jerked one another off in the citrus groves. I fashioned lurid descriptions of tits and ass. That's when I preened and concealed, my guardian angel having long since blown off on the wind. Too weak to thrust bridges of personal shame over the abyss, I snatched Jungian sex shadows flickering on the canyon walls. I relished what I despised. Drawn now exclusively to men, I chewed my fists. I stared into sphincters; many were as sweet as freshly split figs. I did not then intend to murder.

3.

My watch said there was plenty of time for pleasure, guilt, and renunciation. I was still young. Tumid cock heads spurted over my eyes. The worst I could get then was clap. No one thought of AIDS, those piranha-toothed viruses fixing their incisors along your colon's blood-rich capillary seams, overwhelming the castle, crashing its towers in a soup laced with carcinoma flower petals.

4.

"You look cool," says a stranger. "I'm Mona Lisa," I laugh. "In truth, I'm an iron goblet brimming arsenic-laced wine. If I seem facile, forgive me." I fill two glasses with hemlock, one for the man I crave, the other for the one I loathe. "You choose."

5.

A tire-iron in the hands of a gay-basher with a spiny ridge of orange hair like the plume on an Etruscan warrior smashes me. Other punkers pin my arms. I fall. Two ribs on my right side shimmer pain. Marrow neurons blaze. The hoods, screaming "Faggot," run off as a police car wails. Gays leaving the bar are singing, walking in the opposite direction. My mouth is crammed with black thorns. I am bleeding on the macadam.

MOTORCYCLE WITH HITCHHIKER

He thumbs a ride on the wild side of Coast Highway. Though preoccupied with sex, I postpone a climb because of a thrumming bladder. I relieve myself near a creaking oil well against a retaining wall with a mural of Laurel and Hardy and a surfer on a wave. Something scurries. A possum bares its teeth. It's Easter. I want to say adieu before I bleed. I grab a club from a cold fire pit. A crash of bone, a moan. A motorcycle spits. I shift the club from one white hand to the other. The dice are melted sugar cubes. No cards wait on this table. The hiker streams off with his thighs pressed against the leather legs of his biker. Snake's eyes.

BOY WITH A FRAYED SOUL

This boy talks too much, sees nothing. Do I like his aerobic shoes? He's washed his socks. He asks why I'm caking his face. He'll soon be comatose. A finger beneath his tongue quivers like a clarinet reed. Warm saliva, panic, and patina from his anus lather my palm. He holds my balls and slides the other hand beneath my neck, a ruffled feather smelling of ginger. He's wearing sweat socks. A meaty toe protrudes. He's a frayed soul, longing, he says, to saw timber in Montana. I shake lice from his black jacket, rub his groin with witch hazel, his rear with vaseline. I show him the stick I've modified with razor blades. The first cut, or the next, or the next. I snap pictures.

THE SKIN SUIT

He's here for the weekend, stripped, nearly comatose, his cleft chin touching his chest, the stubbled Marine hair cut fresh—since he was coming to see me, as he'd promised. A tiny shaving nick on his cheek. Yes, and the lips as cool as silver, faintly closed—I could insert either my finger or my cock and he would not stir. I've jiggled his anus. My thrill is now supplanted by the bizarre notion that his puckered cleft and inner rugae are textured like grasshopper legs... stubbled and horny. What's under my nail? A carroway seed from the bread he ate, or is it a peanut sliver?

I won't sniff my finger while I'm admiring his white teeth, his closed eyes, his flexible head as limp as a worn sweat sock. The urge to maim stains me like poison. I laugh, for to garrote him now would be like ripping off calendar pages prematurely or eating half-cooked broccoli. I need a calendar "word a day," as they say.

He whispers from the side of his slack mouth: "Where is my Disney wrist watch and the lucky bunny's foot I won in highschool for the broad jump?" If my heart were a well his words would plummet like pebbles forming yellow rings in the stagnant water, down among the snotty condoms, eviscerated toads, the hapless brown chicken too curious for its own good. Last night he said he loved me, though I didn't sleep much, for within minutes drugged on Valium he was snoring, more of a burbling than sawing proverbial chunks of wood. We were both naked. If I had not swallowed his urine he would have soiled my new couch and the happy daisy print with the shepherdess crooks so elegantly positioned on the varnished bare-oak floor.

I want to brag about his flawless skin, but he is not listening. A breath stultifies me—is it mine reversing itself? I want to wear his skin, fitting his eyes over my eyes, his arm pits to mine, his anus, his thighs... Of course, being heavier (almost pudgy) I may burst his seams. But then, recently shucked wet skin is very elastic. Look how the bellies of pregnant women stretch, or males nailed on their backs to racks. Then I see my hunting knife on the table, its haft glittering with Arthurian jewels. The ruby adjoins a gigantic opal and a smoky pearl. A whiff of the orient, of Coleridge.

SWEET SCROTAL TISSUE

I have ingested you and now you lie along my forearm limp, your sheathe as a small globe over your spent glans, bunched as crinkled skin kissed by a pearly tear. You are dreaming of snow, white marble, ropes of sperm wound round with helices gone wild. Sweetness floods my face, sweet scrotal tissue.

THE CANNIBAL

Water flows backwards. I am driving up a hill. Stilettos and tourniquets. Stallion bellies explode among wild ferns. A corpse is speared on a pine. He was humming your favorite song, "The Hills Are Alive With the Sound of Music." Life, you observed, has the clarity of the 23rd Psalm. Your tongue is frozen in glue. "I'll be your wife," you whimpered, "if you hurt me."

Then, you told me of Joachim Kroll who sliced the buttocks of girls into steaks and froze them. When the police arrested him in July 1976, they found a tiny hand garnished with potatoes and carrots boiling in a pot. You thought I'd invented Kroll.

The right cheek of your ass hefted nicely in my hand. Neither your sober logarithms nor your lust's cool geometry could spare you. You flailed a slide rule, bared your teeth, and assumed a parrying position. Oh, you were wild!

PENIS SWATHED IN GREEN SILK

I dress you in wet silk, for your penis looks best displayed against the green, not swathed in it. We can still fly from here—to Timbuctoo, the Alps, Disney World. Your body is a well-tuned instrument. I cram your mouth with my breath: a prelude for *The Sorcerer's Apprentice*. Your belly, thumped, rings a flawed but discernible B Minor. A tear gathers in the slit of your glans, drips on the sheet, near your polished boots. Your nipples are tinged purple. The furnace whirs. A Betty Boop night light casts you in a new position. The neighbor's orange cat shakes its paws on the top of a picket fence. I douse the light.

CHRISTMAS MEMENTOS

1.

I bought the bed sheets on Christmas Eve to please him. A flannel Santa in a toy-crammed sleigh waves at other flannel Santas in toy-crammed sleighs. Bayberry candles permeate the room.

The kid is the type of late adolescent hunk I love. I lap up Tokay laced with acid from his flawless buttock dish. I ream his navel of fuzz. How else should I spend Christmas?

2.

I pass a few camphor-tainted hours visiting my folks. I want to cover their cheeks with blank wooden masks and scribble expressions with colored pens. They forget I'm there as soon as they unwrap their chocolate-covered cherries, don the party hats, and blow their paper whistles. Dad smears chocolate in Mom's face. He's wearing purple pajamas.

Dad's boar's eyes glimmer, illuminating his smirking mouth. He stands next to Mom's hospital chair fondling himself. His pig eyes lust. He even grunts. Mom's mask resembles a gaping fish with scales, a snell, and a hook. She's just landed on the beach.

My sister, earlier, had trimmed a plastic tree which they've knocked off the TV. The branches lay like arms wrenched from sockets. Dad whines that I've sent no Xmas card. They deserve my respect for all they've done for me. There's no end in sight.

I restore the tree, cover Mom's lap with an afghan and throw Dad a paper towel for wiping chocolate dribbles from his chin. My chest feels stuffed with aluminum. The old folks fill their mask eye holes with tears. I tell them I love them, patting their heads. In truth, I would have wrung their necks had Christmas not been so inappropriate for parricide. Thumping my aluminum chest, I leave the house.

3.

"Where will you take me?" asks the youth waiting near the picture window. He admires my bluchers. "I'll lick them," he says, "then follow you down the Yellow Brick Road." On the TV an enormous Pavarotti with a black squash-like head and gapped teeth sings carols in a German cathedral.

"Don't worry, Jake—it is Jake, isn't it? I'm feeling sentimental, having just come from my folks. I predict: You'll die old. You'll probably keel over on a bench outside a public library where you've spent the afternoon staying warm."

4.

We strip and I douse the lights. My fingernails rend his flesh, drawing jewels. "Your blood tastes good," I say. He squeals, turning on his belly. He draws his right leg up. A scattering of black hair garnishes a perfectly puckered anus. I wind holly blent with mistletoe around the sacred hole, grease a slim red bayberry candle, insert, and light it. He lies with his arms and head over the bed. The fat tenor segues from "Adeste Fidelis" to "Silent Night." Killer and victim are entwined on a night of wise men, Aldebaran, and a birth in the straw.

I'M TO BLAME

Have you ever seen a sow grin, or a ewe's saliva go blue while being tupped? Have you watched a sow gnash her farrow, crunching the pink morsels with eclat? Your debaucheries excite this collie. Guilt streams from my hair, chest, limbs, and hands. Royal colors tinged with sun, colors of the huntsman. Pets love you best when you're tickling their comical ears, or whacking their genitals while fondling a Swiss Army knife. Say I'm to blame.

AT THE PLAY: FACES IN A CROWD

1.

Library book cases create a semi-circular fan for folding chairs facing a small acting space. A blue drape sweeps the floor, touching a vivid Turkish carpet on which sits a throne trimmed in red velvet and a pair of end tables. One holds a sheet of parchment, a silver ink well, and a peacock feather pen. On the other is a bowl of tangerines, a large lighted gold candle, and a silver summoning bell. Nearby is a harpsichord.

I feel superior to the puppets around me: A wizened man with hearing aid, wearing ecru polyester pants, a blue shirt with an alligator trademark, and a yachting cap. A middle-aged couple, both with enormous bottoms crammed into scruffy jeans, she gap-toothed, he with a mustache of curls resembling pubic hair. Another ruddy man in his thirties in Polyester pants so tight he has to suck in his breath to keep the buttons from popping. What *is* a poor girl to do?

More puppets: a pair of hirsute, scrawny middle-aged males, left-over flower-children from the days when Laguna was a Timothy Leary haven for transcendentalism freaks and long-haired runaways with mangy, flea-bitten dogs called "Blue," "Spot," and "Basting Spoon." One male, sporting a dirty halo of electrified graying hair, holds a sheaf of pencil-scribbled poems which he scans with his good eye, hoping, so he tells his companion, he'll be invited to read. He evokes scarlet fever scabs and hepatitis drips washed up on a beach poisoning the winkles. Besides a few genteel ladies and gents, there are half a dozen teenagers with tans and tank tops. An unattractive dark-haired youth, callipygous, keeps bobbing in his chair, orchestrated by the withered shrubbery of his brain. Occasionally, he swats something, catches it, then crushes it between his thumb and forefinger. The play is about murder.

2.

A man wearing a white filmy floor-length gown trimmed with pearls and a cincture of glittering metal flakes, with a black lace train which he secures with a white-gloved hand, appears to recorded wolf howls. His black, shoulder-length wig, severely parted with bobby pins, exposes a face layered with white pancake tinted with flesh tones, a beauty spot, and purple grease smeared around his eyes. False lashes. Teal shadows. Lips tinted a livid red/orange. Silver slippers. The Hungarian Countess he portrays bathed in the blood of 700 virgins as a way of maintaining her youth. All this occurred in Transylvania.

SUBURBANITE WASHING HIS CAR

My Saturday auto ritual amazes me: oddly, I am no murderer. As I degrime the hood with lavish suds, the car's blue flanks quiver. A flapping mane rides the soapy crest. I whinny. Blood won't mix with oil. I've always loved good grooming. A pause: instant photos of dead boys, hot coals in my hands. Click, and they're locked in the glove compartment. I sigh. Rain is rare now. I expect nothing beyond tonight's shower of blood. I demolish some showy nasturtiums with a water jet. Jonquils spit back. "Up yours," I laugh, rubbing the car with a chamois. A boy shimmers in a bluebell haze. He's ashamed, he says, being dead. He lifts his T shirt. "See, I'm a ripple of death, a tenant for cold holes and slashes. Moist teeth, death's hood, an incandescence of eyeless sockets in a chrome skull.

KNIFE OR GUN

Lying flat on the ground, trussed, on his back, the dandy Marine asks me why I don't just shoot him. I'd drawn the rawhide shoelace (from his right boot) around his throat, and his words spewed shiny drops of blood. I draw up one of the many smiles I keep in my arsenal: "I don't own a gun," I whisper into his teeth. "Such messes, and you'd flop about like a beetle doing somersaults. You're much too pretty to go that way." I've never shot a man, nor shall I. A gun is wood and steel. Both are extensions of our hands — they throw lethal power far past the sadly limited reach of our fingers. I'm after knowledge. I'd rather cut it out of a body with a blade, curetting so slowly the victim becomes a sybarite of pain. My failures once again shred my wrists. Stop. Stop. I won't write more today. Do you understand?

THE GARDENER

Two of my cauliflowers form heads. The remaining ten have insipid brown florets resembling Queen Anne's Lace. Minuscule black slugs and fecal drippings choke the diseased calyxes. Lettuce, thyme, oregano, and Swiss chard flourish within a plastic barrier. With a spade I unearth cutworms, fat ones with orange mandibles, which I arrange on bricks and slice. My spring garden is in: zucchini, bell peppers, red cabbage, lettuce, tomatoes, and onions. I wear nothing but an old jockstrap. I am kissing the world.

In the front yard a glorious red amaryllis explodes. Moments before, it thrust up as a light green phallus tipped with crimson. We shall have more daffodils. And the roses! Their savory gonadal centers luxuriant with syrup, calyxes for snuffing lives.

BURNED MOUNTAIN SIDE AT SUNSET

A lurid sunset and smoking eucalyptus leaves. The mountain side is seared. At the base acacia flowers droop. The singed mountain warms the cold air rolling in from the sea at dusk. The last wink of the sun's scarlet ball dips below the rim of the world, my chilly chestnut tree, the ribbed ruins of a fashionable gazebo perched above boulders where the seals bellow and slither.

HANDSOME YOUTH SUCKING HIS THUMB

A car cigarette lighter for scorching eyeballs is not enough. A tree branch with protrusions where limbs were is not enough. He will char both nipples off, and still that won't be enough. He'll cut off an ear and wrap it around the head of his own cock and kum and that won't be enough. The chopped off nose lying on a Delft plate, one of a set his mom gave him for Christmas, looks like a pig's —and that is not enough. He dances over his beige condo rug, brushes against his beloved cut glass and china collection in its cherry-wood cupboard, swirls around the violated corpse, thinking he's a child blowing chaff from a milkweed pod ready to burst. And that won't be enough. He thrusts one hand in the boy's mouth and grabs his tongue. His free hand gropes the boy's buttocks, twisting black hairs, yanking them free, rolling them into balls. And this too is not enough. He calls the boy his lover and cradles his dead head and kisses the bruised eyes and swollen lips. Nor is this enough. He withdraws his penis and sits cross legged near the bed. He wads the dead boy's t-shirt, holds it to his own face, sucks out sweat, sucks his own thumb. None of this is enough.

MILKY TEA

He is so naked, young, slightly pot-bellied. His slack flesh is rubber, swollen with rotten pulp beneath a thin external skin. I guess, being exotic, I think of sucking mangoes. Slurping such flesh requires no teeth. I'd scrape a monkey's paw over his face and draw blood. He's the tint of milky tea, particularly along his neck where the ligature was, traversing the neck cord, the intimate warm spot of his throat. I can't stop kissing him no matter how icy his body, no matter how white and perfect his teeth.

SANTA ANA VIEWS

Soot drips from raunchy sycamores into litter-filled planters in downtown Santa Ana. Noon shimmers on two Latinas admiring wedding gowns in the window of a shop blaring music from cheap stereo systems. The bridal mannequins resemble Barbie dolls. Both are missing fingers. The train of one is held by a plump brown plastic child in a pink dress. The women seem to be mother and daughter. Both are short with wide backs and bottoms. They hold hands as they jabber.

I near the court house, the tallest building in the city. Two shirtless youths with black jackets adorned with bugle-bead, screaming firebirds loiter outside a beer bar featuring a spider's web. One youth has hard pecs and nipples. The "Cantina" sign of faded barber pole stripes spins above them as they enter. Death, I assume, relates unrelated parts.

Though I could never live in the barrio, I might buy a clapboard, single-story house there, one with torn screens, fractured porch dowels, and a litter of wrecked children's toys and rusted patio furniture in the front yard, and rent it to undocumented workers, enlarging the County tax base and fostering cheap labor. I've stashed money towards this goal. I've also been learning Spanish, which is no problem since all my life I've lived in proximity to Latinos. You can't be an Orange Countyian otherwise, unless you dwell in white communities with gateposts. Santa Ana is the nearest thing we have to Tia Juana or Calcutta.

I'm in a swirl of uniformed police, of men and women, largely young, shaking ash from nervous cigarettes, of judges and lawyers emerging from limos in restricted parking spaces, of vendors selling hot dogs and cold drinks from aluminum push carts. My image reflects from a pool of liver-colored water. No matter how much they try for special effects this court house is grim. My face is grim.

Why do I come here? Though I am feverish, I feel no different than I did an hour ago when I parked on Main Street adjacent to some tiny houses inhabited by Latino lawyers and bail bondsmen. Eventually I shall be caught, shackled, and escorted to the eighth floor of this building where the only egress is by elevator and the air is foul. I attend the trial of a woman who in post-partum distress placed her baby in her driveway and ran her Dodge van over its head, smashing it into praline. Like me, she is trapped. She has, it appears, a sympathetic judge and, whining, has hidden her hands allowing both halves of her face to stream remorse. I am no eviscerator, though I have carved men into angels. All that I feel (I'm not confessing) is subterranean. I won't weep. I'll grin if the guards beat me. Guilt is a curse.

YOUTH AND CAR STALLED
IN SNOWY RAVINE

Syllables of foam. My teeth are crumbling into talc. Your body is mere skin and cartilage. You are so young. If I strangle you, forgive me. I wallow in psychic ditches of filth.

You were standing waist deep in that horrendous storm, outside the cabin door where inside I had taken pills to ease the torture of missing you. Pearls were your eyes. A red crayfish your nose. Abalone shells your ears. Did you shout? It was four a.m., wasn't it, and the snow was streaming? The fireplace was full of embers and the smell of wool.

Your car crashed and slid through a web of ponderosa saplings into a ravine. Only the maroon top was visible in the snow drift. We hired a truck to pull you out. Somehow you escaped, and here you are.

We shut the cabin door only after first pushing snow aside. A scrub jay screamed from a cranny in a spruce. I was jealous, thinking you had tricked on me. I was crazy. It didn't matter whether I lived or died, without you.

I did not think you'd find me on Sunday. For five days I've sweltered and tossed. Twice in a vision you stood naked by my bed. Twice I arose immersed in bitter fog, ice a blue shine everywhere, no fire in the grate, the blizzard lashing the roof, and you were absent. I knew then how bricks scream, and stones clang careening down a glacier.

I'll sing for you, snow bird, and I'll eat your sweat, your ashes, and your soul.

THE VISITING TENOR

We abandoned the visiting tenor in the desert. He had clasped us while chomping gluttonously on dates. He swallowed most of the seeds. Finally, when he had to pee, we drove off in our Escort indifferent to his survival skills in those livid sunset wastes.

We stopped in Julian, drawn to the ramshackle buildings and the barber shop. I needed a haircut. You, friend, misunderstood, I think, pressured by our house-guest's needs, and the obnoxious flow of easy farts as he relaxed in my recliner pontificating about Caruso, Bjerling, and Melchior, clipping hairs from his nose. His lyric tones sweetened, passing through his grain-yellow paunch globules via reverse osmosis. He'd sing for us, if we chose. True, the only California boy he'd been able to attract was a doper desperate for a warm stove.

The barber pronounced my hair too brittle. He was from Seattle, a city we'd visited, booked a room in, and left when we found shit stains on the sheets. No small talk. He wasn't to blame for our modest disaster. Wisps of my gray hair on the floor, silky, much like my dad's. You waited in a defunct plastic chair, thumbing *Mad Magazine*. I started scratching my head—psoriasis?

"You will fetch him, won't you?" said the barber. "He's a regular customer." "That'll do," I exclaimed, rising. The barber's meaty hand smelled of chloroform. "Help me," I said. But you were already out of reach, near the door, counting cigars. You turned, smiling, and sang an aria from "Tosca." A displeased sun-burned visage glowered at the window, tentacles with suction cups.

COUSINS

Blood drools from the lips of the cousins lying face to face in the snow. Four substantial shrouded haystacks. Sheltering Norway pines. No one can see me. A woman in a farm house window, a woman with gray plaits drawing back her flimsy curtains. Chicadees sweep the wispy smoke emerging from the chimney. Lowing cattle wait to be milked. Three boys in mackinaws cut figure eights over a pasture ice rink.

When the sun sinks, dim rodent forms leap in the sumac, gathering, avid for meat, avid for my departure.

I kick the crisp bristles of frozen timothy blades, crack my heel against surface ice swollen in a wheel rut. A single red maple leaf, an elfin mitten, twirls on its tree, perverse.

To open my car trunk I dislodge ice from the lock. An onslaught of Arctic wind crackles like frozen bed sheets on a wire line. There they lie, my sweeties: my farm lads have pissed red, which I was not expecting.

Hertz will conclude I've damaged their car. In a fix, you must always plead ignorance — I'd never inspected the trunk, had no need to open it, et cetera. Yet, there's bloody ice. You know how sugary it is frozen into blent reds segueing into whites, crazed window glass or transparent laminations. The interior of the car is pristine.

Since I loved the boys, I place them facing one another in a drift. Snow spews red-tinged foam into the air. Here death is not disgusting, is as pleasant as swan's down. The cousins wear frost diadems and ice-drop tiaras.

Once more, in enormous flakes, snow welters. As I scurry to my car, someone (is it God?) shouts in a black voice. A wolverine dashes forth, poises, rubs its paws, and locks its jaws on a throat. Other wood forms, dark large round creatures, bunch ravenous nearby.

PART THREE:

SNAPSHOTS FOR A TRIAL

POLAROID OF ROBERT POWERS

They found Robert Powers' body decomposed, jammed into a trash bag near the El Toro Marine base. Investigators identified his tattoos: "Dazed and Confused," "Merlin the Magician", and a red rose. The prosecution produced twenty-one of my photos of Powers nude, appearing dead. They'd ransacked my house. In one picture was a white sock with blue stripes matching one stuffed up his anus. On the "Scorecard," found in my car, with sixty-one coded entries for my reputed victims, the prosecutor avers that "MC HB Tattoo" refers to Powers, a sailor, last seen in Huntington Beach, who loved tattoos. Judge McCartin is irritated when my attorneys seek to have these grisly pictures withheld from the jurors as prejudicial to me. We fail. The jury sees a rotting nude youth with hands and feet bound and eyeballs and nipples concentrically scorched with a cigarette lighter.

SNAPSHOTS AT MY TRIAL

"It's your can of worms," I want to shout to the voyeurs. I nod to a couple of women I trained for computers and to a middle-aged queen in a cashmere sweater famous for his blows. I grin at the mother of a victim (aged thirteen) who as a Niobe in tears jams her clammy ass daily into a chair near mine. Today she's brought her aging mother. Will parent survive the prosecutor's grisly visual aids? The butchered grandson in "living" color? They wheel my own senile parents in. Special dispensation from His Honor. Mom and Dad don't know me, but the media love my dutiful kissing of their white, bobbing heads.

The media so far have merely noticed my trial, "The most expensive in history." You'd think I'd be a celebrity, with my smile splashed everywhere. But, sixteen murders—and possibly sixty-one, they aver, are too repetitious and gory. Readers require a less persistent *stretto*. If I had killed real estate developers or TV stars I'd be generic. Drifters and "queers" deserve their fate. In such homophobic times, the public is bemused. Yet, though I'm forty-four I'm still handsome, with hair cropped short, a neat blue shirt open at the throat, faded jeans. I've been in solitary for six years eating eruptive beans washed down with Diet Pepsi.

April 5: The night of my arrest. Why was I so stupid? Meandering the freeways with a garroted, still warm, Marine, beside me in the passenger seat. Though he was nude and my own pants were down, I insisted that I had found him on the berm and was rushing him to an emergency room. I had wiped his genitals with a sock as best I could.

I have three high-priced lawyers, all at public expense, and two bailiffs. One is a blond. The other is a Latino with thighs like a horse and a cleft chin. The prosecuting

85

attorney was a tennis star. I want to sleep with him. The judge wears a collar for a bad vertebra. Three ceramic monkeys of evil crouch along his bench. Two plants and a smiling bloodhound. His Honor rarely eats lunch and bestows stiff sentences.

I've pled innocent, which, of course, I am. For this is Hollywood and I am the King of Siam.

Busby Berkeley girls shuffle on in drag, brushing mutilated corpses with pastel flags. The colored mayhem photos are much enlarged. Only two males on the jury. There's a hush. I dash off notes, gazing rarely at my grisly handiwork, bones with fleshy scraps attached, guts, butt views showing scrotum and penis excised. Why didn't they scrub the boys? A severed scalp flung over a face. Vivisected hearts. Ligature marks on throats and ankles. Tree branches thrust up fundaments. A rat's heart beats 120 times per minute, so I'm told. I feel "cool." Consultations with the judge. Arguments at the bench with the jury absent. I'm sour wine, a pewter apple, a candle about to snuff itself in its own wax. A break for lunch.

EXECUTION DREAM-SCAPE

The snowy San Gabriels. Strange, for it never snows there, or rarely. I observed the scene this morning during my daily walk on the roof of the jail, where I am incarcerated without letters, without bail. I've sued to have video porn brought in. They don't take me seriously, say I should read the Rev. Schuller or Danielle Steele.

Yes, I said "snow": Young officers escort me to a mountain. I'm on the bare back of a flawless white stallion. I wear only a g-string. We halt, and I suck off the officer of my choice. Then he tosses a rope over a Ponderosa branch. Fluttering snow covers my shoulders. As he tightens the noose I spew forth the officers' sperm which freezes on my chest. My feet kick out. My neck snaps. I'm an ice dove! They don't see my smile until they cut me down. My head on its stem slips forward, a snapped calla lily.

A MOTHER

The short, plump mom with eyes like gray anemones, frizzed hair, and a spiral notebook sits near the defendant's table. The oak railing burns with black pomegranates, hibiscus, ashen cypress twigs, calyxes of lizard tongues, and strawberry blooms of pain. I am Satan facing her.

She flings burning silica at my head. She would glaze a window with granite to bring back her son, to kiss his cherry lips. What she craves is, of course, hopeless. She's reduced to unsheathing claws of rage. Her hoarse breath emits barbed fish vertebrae, ridiculous harpoons that never penetrate.

When I first faced her, I smiled. Even today a sore spot remains on my nape where her gaze burned through. Wearing a starched collar doesn't help.

On most days a fat man with a nose like a scimitar sits holding her hand. They've been estranged ever since their son's head was found off a quay, the skeleton in manzanita twenty miles down the coast. Now, they report, the trial has restored their marriage. There were terrible fights, neither accepting blame for having ejected the son as a truculent drop-out, doper, and tramp.

This mom is the most persistent of a dozen mothers on the witness stand. They see snapshots of couches, living room floors, and cars where their boys died. They see the final terrifying beds of rock, shrub, and sand, with the warm bodies knifed, bruised, and trashed. We show them frozen smiles—no snapped face expresses anguish. Fathers, in public, learn that their sons were homosexual. The dads resemble pilots on solo flights during snowstorms; they don't know where they are. The mothers always glare at me, the fathers never do.

This mom loves being interviewed, especially during trial breaks when she stands near her front-row seat, dripping tears. Her train careens through flooded landscapes. A lilac shrub of death roots inside her. When I snuffed her son, I snuffed her as well.

During the autopsy photos, she hides her face. "If the wounds had been ante-mortem," drones a pathologist wearing a red reindeer tie (he's been flown in from Hawaii), "there would have been blood in the eyes. The victim was dead when the killer grabbed the cigarette lighter from the dashboard, opened the eyelids, and seared those concentric rings." Ditto for the charred nipples. "Yes, the victim was dead, of alcohol, benzedrine, and garroting. Moreover, blood in the genital area shows that the testicles and half the penis were excised ante-mortem..."

The prosecuting attorney appears solicitous, but shakes the guilt tree, dropping over-ripe fruit in my lap, smiling. Perhaps he imagines the bereaved families licking his oxfords. I don't know. His winsome, ingenue boy lawyer manner is misleading; for he gets convictions.

I feel quite safe in my charmed circle, immune from the spectators slapping massive detestations like furious lava combs against the cool, honey-colored bar of justice. Yes, someone could shoot me, though most people are cowards. "Courageous" males shaft *sotto voce* obscenities at the breaks, sure that I can't retaliate.

I keep smiling, appearing as though I'm having raspberries and cream with my secretaries at morning coffee break.

I scribble notes in legal pads. I sketch the mothers. I sketch sheep dogs playing with boys. I draw valentines with arrows shot through them. I jot facts to discuss with my lawyers. I sketch Santas with hard ons. I've always wanted my own private cemetery, with a portrait photo set into the headstone of each victim's grave, to remind me of the fragility of love, of how once you've invited someone in they soon split. No one inks your contract. When you see them sucking their thumbs, you drug them and plow them under.

This agricultural image reminds me of germination and the trees from which corpses dangle like red death flags. I *feel* all of these bodies. Their hearts pound, their blood congeals as I traverse forests choked with leaves.

PET SCAN BRAIN PHOTOS

They project slides of my brain with hot spots as brilliant as those in Tia Juana paper flowers. The spots, however, are far more mysterious, resembling figures in a Turkish carpet arranged in a tondo on a flat, black exhibit board. One I recall reputedly shows evidence of a head injury when I was two. The Brain Imaging Professor "slices" the rear portion of my brain, filling up the lower space of the photo with an oversized, feral head, powerful front shoulders adorned with a livid square inside an orange circle patterned with risers like those in Aztec designs. From the rear, haunches spring and a misty figure resembles an Aztec cockerel. The faster flowing the eddies of blue, yellow, orange and red, the psychiatrist explains, the more likely it is that brain damage caused my sexual disorders. His technology, in a sense, rapes my brain, imaging my personal hypothalamus.

My lawyers are taking a risk via presenting these photos, tacitly saying I am guilty but asking that I be pardoned (and treated) for my cerebellum flowers. Few courts yet accept such evidence. I feel like saying "mumbo jumbo" but hold my tongue. Our best hope is that during our appeal a higher court will allow these scans. I am not sanguine.

PIRANESIAN VIEWS

Piranesi's Renaissance prisons are peaceful. He keeps you climbing, the stone risers worn by shod feet moving inexorably to the torture galleries. He loved "the pear," that hollow metal fruit used for killing homosexuals. You inserted it up a rectum, then with a screw twisted it open until the victim screamed and shreds of flesh sprang forth like jelly fish filaments. A moist sphincter (a rose bud) betrayed you as Uranian. As the poet Miklós Radnóti observed: "Little buds / whose noses are always wet don't open / when the sky is filled with whistling."

Moreover, these "perverts" always thought they were shards of blue Egyptian tomb glass and by assuming frog postures hoped to hop away. Their whistling priest-tormentors dragged them back and crushed them!

I find Piranesi's drawings sublime. Once I had half a dozen matted, framed, and hung along my bedroom wall, so that immediately on entering they drew you in. Where are they now? All of my possessions are "dispossessed," if you'll excuse the levity, and are in my sister's garage, packed with all else I owned of any value, all towards my being found innocent, on appeal, of these reputed crimes and released.

If I'm gassed, will I float off like a ghost? If I've had nothing will I ever have anything again? What I owned is "sicklied o'er" with slimy maggots and snails, mildew, and the dissolution of wood and paper into dust. You may wrench Piranesi's images from the man, but never from his brain. I'm on a rack.

DUAL SNAPSHOT WITH BLEMISHES

I've survived another day. The moon shines through my solitary window brighter than before. My brain sliced like a potato on a cutting board reassembles itself. Fog drifts past the jail, obliterating the moon. Down the corridor a man is whining. Another is saying his beads. They grab away everything here, even my belt and shoelaces. I will shortly emerge into an exotic landscape crammed with blazing paper flowers. I meditate on Dennis Nilsen, Britain's serial killer who was arrested on Feb. 9, 1983 and imprisoned for life.

No capital punishment in the UK. Is he a brother? He was a homosexual. Nilsen scribbles poems, letters, and accounts of the deaths of fifteen young men. In the army he cut meat with a skilled surgeon's eye. He dismembered drugged victims in a bathtub, with the faucet running. He boiled heads on his apartment range to make disposal easier. Other bones he incinerated on bonfires. No neighbor was drawn either by the smell of burning flesh or by the stench of corpses rotting beneath floorboards. He spent a fortune on room deodorant sprays. No one at the Government Employment Office where he was admired (as I was at my work) suspected him. He compartmentalized his lives. Think: Who truly knows your private acts? When you probe your hemorrhoids? Jert masturbation rhythms? How many strangers have seen your genitals afloat in the bath?

Nilsen threw tires on the pyre with his corpses, concealing the odors of sizzling livers and exploding eyeballs. When he flushed body parts down his toilet (he lived on the 4th floor), he clogged the plumbing. When the toilets overflowed, he was apprehended. A lonely fellow, he was handsome (as I am), and had a mongrel Bleep who padded around the apartment while his master killed for "company." Nilsen feared being alone. None of his tricks, alive, stayed longer than for a single night of sex, pop music, and dope. He felt sorry for himself on holidays, particularly on New Years' Eve. He was never invited to parties.

To guarantee that his victims would never leave, he stashed them beneath his living room floor. Once rigor mortis passed and the bodies were again flaccid (I had always assumed that rigor mortis was permanent) he'd disinter them, prop them in chairs, and regale them with their favorite rock and roll hits. He especially liked Lori Anderson's "Superman," which he even sang in his sleep. When the dead faces turned fecal, Nilsen covered them with plastic bags.

I want to be clear. I am not Nilsen's brother, nor am I his keeper. After my murders, I was like an anxious dog dragging its paws over a door. I craved to dump the remains, for the dead offend my need for personal order. Are you surprised? It's an issue of esthetics, not morality: you can't light up love blossoms on a bloated stomach or on an crotch smeared with blood, piss, and shit. I dumped these noisome carcasses onto freeway ramps, rarely looking back. And the snapshots the police produced as evidence—I clicked those before the boys were really dead, as a record of beauty in transition to decay. This, friend, is the story of your life, as it is of mine.

After dumping a body, I'd drive for hours, allowing just enough time to shower, eat breakfast, dress, and go to work. I was one of the best computer experts in the business, and traveled as far east as Ann Arbor, Michigan, for consultations.

The blazing darts of approaching cars lit up the corpse in the passenger seat—thrills, for, couldn't they tell the difference between a body slumbering and a body morbid? Much of the earth we tread is neutral space. Corpse-whiffs are of no more consequence than clouds rippling through a transparent sky.

Both I and the police snap photos, including shots of manzanita near the freeway, or of dumpsters where bluebottle flies gorge on sugary blood. You must leave evidence of your imagination and style, always. I am no slimy lizard gulping it's prey without first arranging place settings of silver, candles, crystal, and quality napkins. Sliced gonads on lettuce leaves. Protocol, protocol. Death's ecru is so subtle it leaves you breathless. Oh, give me autumn leaves dipped in silver! Oh, give me John Keats!

MOMS KNOW BEST

Once the aluminum Merecedes motors are melted into
reusable ingots   After Pilar Wayne's (she's John Wayne's
widow) brass bird cages are smashed and the birds are
smears   Once the soiled briefs of my murder victims are
burned   I'll still feast with wolves on doped young drifters
along Coast Highway, thumbs out, hoping for a mouthful
of raven feathers and an obscene, quick fuck   You moms
know what I mean—skuas flopping in over the icebergs with
their vicious beaks and claws rattling   Your sons were
gorgeous in their uniforms   You were so proud

JAIL CELL TABLE TOP WITH LEXICONS

During my five-year pre-trial incarceration, I could tan only so much *putrescent* mouse skin, and I hated needle work. After struggling with awls and leather trimmed for shoes, I would stand before my window (I was lucky to have one) my breath steaming the murky glass. I suspended cardboard over my bed and played darts. I always won. The guards, disgusted, soon deprived me of awl, leather, and last. They refused me a word processor. They refused me the novels I wanted: Hubert Selby Jr.'s *Last Exit to Brooklyn*; anything by John Rechy; Burroughs' *Naked Lunch*; William Joyce's *First Born of an Ass*; Jim Thompson. I was even ready to tackle William Faulkner and Henry James. I reminded the warden that I always won school prizes for reading. Note the connections between my verbal and computer skills. I've always been smart, and proud of it. By *interdigitating* these I could be useful to the prison administration—clerical labor for free.

The warden laughed and produced well-thumbed cheap novels with the covers ripped off so as to diminish the erotic quotient; for many of these horrid books were of the Mystery/Romance variety. They sneered when I asked for works published by gay presses. They agreed to lexicons, for they're *utilitarian*. They produced a used two volume edition of the Oxford English Dictionary. I had to pay for it. My sister gave me "a word a day" calendar. I vow that at my death I'll have the largest vocabulary of any doomed man in U.S. penal history. I am, as you might assume, a crossword puzzle freak.

I still jot words into notebooks: *borborygmic*: many of my youths experienced rumblings caused by intestinal gas. *trichologist*: would the prosecution hire specialists to match hairs found in my car with those of victims? *manumission*: mine would probably come only with my execution.

Metagrobolized: my lawyers perpetually mystified me via their abstruse strategies; what *arcane* reasons, for example, led them to keep me from testifying in my own defense? *speciesism*: I would prove through my word-lust that the popular image of murderers as retarded was false.

I would, if I had to, leave all but one of my dictionaries behind. I'd carry one, bound in white leather and stamped in gold, as a final testament, on the walk to the green chamber. Better than toting the Authorized King James Version.

Where will all these words I've crammed into my brain go? To an urn in a columbarium? Will they evaporate through the universe condensing during mystical hours, separately, for distressed young men? They'd be merry company.

ARITHMETIC

Pose me before a retaining wall fronting a beautiful beach etched with the names of my victims. I will tell you, up front, that though they lived I believe I did not kill them. For I was much younger then and loved my "accidents" to appear chancy, graceful. I loved the benign smiles, although their lips and eyes were sealed with a vicious, opaque resin. If I apologize now, I'll be a lousy Indian giver. I can't restore what's snuffed, with or without interest, the wampum included in the original deal. You can add, multiply, and divide, right? You know the difference between ordinal (male) and cardinal (female) numbers. Without flinching you solve work and distance problems. You are a whiz at fractions. So, tote up those images on the retaining wall. Don't be stupid. Think of AIDS. Think about strangulation and sodomy. What about that. Who are the lucky ones?

FINAL VICTIM AS A NOVA IN ETERNITY

Love, I kissed your body during our last tryst eight years ago, before I killed you. I've been meaning to describe for you the galaxy I've invented here through this prison window, after lights out, after the moon blatantly spatters the California sky. You are a Nova. You glow like a bead of radium on the breast of a Nubian prince.

I'm sick of tomorrow, and the petty ways it creeps—Shakespeare said that, didn't he? I am tufts of hair and an assemblage of bones glued with a solder requiring no heat. You are probably rubbing your thumb against your curvaceous index finger, and thinking of me, how I loved biting you. Your wine glass is empty, fill it. You've made me forget my trope, yes, my special galaxy featuring you. I can erase it with a blink. But I don't want to, for you still excite me. I am your constant moon and you are here warm, ecstatic, loving me. Believe that, no matter how they denigrate me. Love me.

CODA

SCORECARD

Prosecutors maintain that a paper with 61 entries found in the murderer's car trunk at the time of his arrest in May 1983 is a death list, with entries dating back to late 1971. Killer claims that the list refers to friends of his and to old roommates. The initial capitalized entries match the killer's list as published in a local newspaper. As the grisly remains surfaced, the prosecutors matched the killer's clues to the victims.

1. STABLE. W. J. W., 30, of Long Beach, found dead at bottom of a ravine in Orange County, next to the Ortega Highway. Suffered from acute alcohol intoxication.

2. ANGEL. Unsolved.

3. EDS. A Marine from Camp Pendelton, found at a freeway interchange. Strangled. Sock stuffed up anus.

4. HARI KARI. Unsolved.

5. AIRPLANE HILL. A "John Doe" found on Airplane Hill in Huntington Beach. Sodomized.

6. MARINE DOWN. Unsolved.

7. VAN DRIVEWAY. Unsolved.

8. 2 IN 1 MV TO PL: Unsolved.

9. TWIGGIE. J. D., 19, of Cypress, California, found near freeway in S. Orange County. Nude except for T-shirt. 4' tree branch shoved up his anus.

10. VINCE M. Found at bottom of ravine in San Bernardino mountains. Shoeless. Sock stuffed into anus and genitals mutilated. Hands severed from body.

11. WILMINGTON. Another "John Doe" found in Wilmington. Nude with sock up anus.

12. LB MARINA. Unsolved.

13. PIER 2. T. L. B., found on a pier in Long Beach Harbor, strangled.

14. DIABETIC. Not connected to unsolved murder.

15. SKATES. W. J. L., 17, found floating in surf at Sunset Beach. Wooden surveyor's stake stuffed up anus. Was seen the day before boarding a bus en route to a roller skating rink carrying new skates. Suffocated.

16. PORTLAND. Unsolved.

17. NAVY WHITE. Unsolved.

18. USER. Unsolved.

19. PARKING LOT. C. D. K., 19, was seen leaving parking lot with killer. Head found near a jetty. Skeletal remains, lacking hands, found months later near a Marine base.

20. DEODORANT. R. P., 16, found near Hollywood Freeway. Known as heavy deodorant user. Strangled.

21. DOG. G. D. R., 13, found next to body of #20. He was visiting relatives and had gone to a park to seek his lost dog. Strangled.

22. TEEN TRUCKER. E. L. M., from Alabama, found near Salton Sea, California. Emasculated, with branch stuffed up anus.

23. IOWA. Unsolved.

24. 7TH STREET. F. W. R., found along San Diego Freeway. Body redressed, except for shoes. Sock up anus. Strangled. Body ejected from moving car.

25. LAKES MC. J. W. G., from Florida, found in Big Bear area. Wore military clothing and told people he was a Marine. Body found without head or legs. Emasculated.

26. MC LAGUNA. D. R. E., Marine, found near a dead-end street in Laguna Beach. Sodomized. Bite marks. Strangled.

27. GOLDEN SAILS. V. G. J., found on Pacific Coast Highway. Shoes and socks missing. Strangled.

28. EUCLID. H. M. S., Marine, found on freeway on-ramp, Anaheim. Emasculated. Strangled with his own shoelaces.

29. HAWTH OFF HEAD. "John Doe," found April 22, 1973. Torso on Wilmington. Right leg on Terminal Island Freeway, Long Beach. Head at 7th St. and Redondo in Long Beach. Left leg found behind Broom Hilda's Bar in Sunset Beach. Strangled. Emasculated.

30. 76. "John Doe" No. 299, found in a dumpster behind Union 76 Station in Long Beach. Arms severed at the shoulders, legs at hip joints. Head severed. Only head, left leg, and torso recovered. Sock in body cavity.

31. 2 IN 1 HITCH. Unsolved.

32. BIG SUR. G. G. S., found in Laguna Hills. Missing socks and shoes. Cause of death: acute drug intoxication.

33. MARINE HEAD BP. A. M. A., a Marine, found near Interstate 5. Head and hands severed. Large object stuffed up anus.

34. EXPLETIVE DELETED. F. J. P., disappeared in December, 1988. Last seen at Ripples, a gay bar, in Long Beach.

35. FRONT OF RIPPLES. Unsolved.

36. MARINE CARSON. A. K. E., Marine, found along South Orange County Parkway. Strangled.

37. NEW YEAR'S EVE. H. M. H., found in Santiago Canyon. Eyes and genitals mutilated with an automobile cigarette lighter. Emasculated.

38. WESTMINSTER DATE. B. J. B., 15, of Santa Ana, disappeared after dating a girl in Westminster.

39. JAIL OUT. G. R. P., found near San Diego Freeway, shortly after being released from Orange County Jail for a misdemeanor violation. Emasculated. Stab wound to heart. A jail-release form in his pocket.

40. MARINE DRUNK OVERNIGHT SHORTS. H. C. R., found on San Diego Freeway ramp. Wearing only shorts. Left nipple burned with auto cigarette lighter. Cause of death: alcohol and drug poisoning.

41. CARPENTER. Unsolved.

42. TORRANCE. C. R. A., found in San Bernardino County.

Left nipple mutilated with cigarette lighter. Suffocated.

43. MCDUMP HB SHORT. Unsolved.

44. 2 IN 1 BEACH. G. A. D. and his friend R. J. N., last seen on foot near their homes in Buena Park area. D found on Garden Grove Freeway on-ramp. Nude and emasculated. Thrown from moving vehicle. Strangled. N's body found next day in Angeles National Forest, in a ravine. Sodomized. Suffocated or strangled. Sand on DuVaul linked him to Nelson.

45. HOLLYWOOD BUS. L. R. W., found in San Bernardino Mountains. Missing socks, shoes, and underwear. Paper stuffed up anus. Cause of death: pneumonia due to aspiration.

46. MC HB TATTOO. P. J. T., a Marine, found in a trash bag, nude, on dead-end street in El Toro. Had large tattoo on arm. Death caused by acute intoxication.

47. OXNARD. Unsolved.

48. PORTLAND ECK. "John Doe," Oregon, found near Interstate 5, Oregon. Strangled.

49. PORTLAND DENVER. S. O. M., found near Interstate 5, Salem. Nude. Sodomized. Strangled.

50. PORTLAND BLOOD. D. C. M., found near Interstate 5, Oregon. Sodomized. Bludgeoned 31 times on back of head.

51. PORTLAND HAWAII. T. T. L., found near Wilsonville, ORE. Re-dressed. Sock up anus. His small tote bag marked "Hawaii" found. He was last seen hitchhiking in a shirt with

"Hawaii" printed on it.

52. PORTLAND RESERVE. J. S. A., found on Interstate 5, near Medford, Oregon. Nude, toothbrush shoved up anus. Sodomized. Strangled.

53. PORTLAND HEAD. H. B. W., found near Wilsonville, Oregon. Lacking shoes and socks. Thrown from moving vehicle.

54. GR 2. P. D. S. and A. C. A., two cousins, found together in field near Grand Rapids, Michigan, where they were attending a horticulture convention. Genitals exposed. Asphyxiated by choking. Schoenborn found nude. Amway pen stuffed up anus. Strangled.

55. SD DOPE. L. M. C., found in a remote area of San Diego County. No clothes with skeletal remains.

57. HIKE OUT LB BOOTS. A. R. T., found in traffic lane of Interstate 5, near Mission Viejo. Left nipple burned with auto cigarette lighter. Boot lace missing from left hiking boot. Dumped from a moving vehicle. Drug poisoning.

58. ENGLAND. Unsolved.

59. OIL. Unsolved.

60. DART 405. J. M. J., found at a freeway interchange. Nude, except for pants pulled down below his waist. Emasculated and sodomized. Suffocated.

61. WHAT YOU GOT. Unsolved.

SNAPSHOTS FOR A

SERIAL KILLER

THE PLAY

FOR A SINGLE PERFORMER

Robert Peters

*[STAGE DARK. MIX OF SCHUBERT'S "LULLABY" AND THE
ROLLING STONES' "PAINT IT BLACK." SIMPLE STAGE SET
WITH SMALL TABLE, COUCH, ETC. THE ACTOR, C. THIRTY,
APPEARS IN TIGHT JEANS, LEATHER JACKET WITH STUDS.]*

My Mustang's a great car. My leather jacket is great.
Bought it four years ago at a great S/M leather store in San
Francisco. My stash of pills is great. *[SEES YOUTH IN
AUDIENCE]:* Hey you, lover boy. Your haircut is great.
But you've muddied your great boots. Come on up here.
[PAUSES.] Get in my car. We'll rev north past these
sleeping condos and oil wells. *[HE IMITATES REVVING
MOTOR.]* You've got strong fingers, lover boy. Sure, that's
a gay bar. I'd say you were straight. "To each his own,"
as Bette Davis, or was it Gene Tierney, said. I'd like to feel
your cock. Pop open the glove compartment. Are you
stupid, or what? Just click the button. The pills are yours,
Tom. It is Tom, isn't it? From Iowa? More pills? I want
you to **F L Y**, man! *[MORE REVVING SOUNDS.]* Tom, flex
a muscle. The nipples of your raspberry tits are like hard
cherry pits. You don't dig my rhyme? Here, I'll tip back
your seat. Relax. Shut those eyes. I'm the horny witch of
the west. There's spit on your chin. Here's spit in your eye.
Sleep. *[STOPS CAR. MIMES DRAGGING BODY TO THE SIDE
OF THE ROAD.]* You're anyone I please. Be Ted, be Chris,
be Ben, be Randy. *["PAINT IT BLACK" UP. LIGHTS DOWN.]*

[TO AUDIENCE]: As a boy I often lay in the orange groves,
gazing up at hawks rebuffing the winds. I've always liked
nature. I was active in the Sierra Club, going on outings,
buying calendars. I even wrote letters to rescue elephants,
seals, and whales.

Yes, where were we? My boyhood in the citrus groves. I
fetched toys, fire trucks, erector sets, and a toy GI Joe whose

113

plastic ass I never tired of kissing and fondling. I even made a little anus for him with a nail.

One morning when I was twelve I found sticky stuff all over my belly. Since I was compulsively neat, I asked my friend Timmy Reed if I should see a doctor. He whipped off a batch of his own, so I would know.

At school, whether I was popular or not didn't matter. Thistles rang changes on my sadness. A wood dove flew to my shoulder. On icy nights, the citrus groves were crammed with smudge pots. The San Gabriel mountains glazed with snow. I loved those mountains. I thrilled to the pulse of a wren as my hand crushed its skull.

[TAKES A ROSE FROM THE TABLE.] Mom's not expecting anything for Mother's Day, so she'll be surprised. We're not a demonstrative family. The best presents, Mom always says, are those you give yourself. How's that for an onanistic view of barter, appreciation, and exchange? If you were honest, most of you sitting out there would feel the same.

Alzheimers has clobbered Mom and Dad. A few years ago Sis and I didn't see any signs; we were too busy to notice. In general, I could never please Mom. An analyst would say I loved her too much. Simplistic. Yet, I still get goose bumps when she sings Glen Miller tunes and bakes apple pies with brown sugar crumbs on top.

Like most women of her generation she hated sex. Locked between dad's legs, she found the music harsh, for there was none. I very much want to confuse you. That's as much of a trip as biting your tits off.

The conjunction of Mom's and Dad's parts was harsh: a

114

smelly bone rammed her flower and the grey souls of snails snuffed her screams. That's when Dad's load sent pallid fishy missionaries up Mom's tubes. One little squiggler rode oarless and rudderless through that Congo of darkness, piercing Mom's egg, creating me.

Later today, I'll surprise Mom in the midst of dishing up pork chops, beets, and mashed potatoes. She'll be wearing a sloppy apron. Her unkempt hair will fly out in strands, and she'll have, as usual, burned the meat. I'll hold this rose to her face. "Mom." She'll be startled, sigh, put down the serving dish, take the rose, and kiss me. *[FLINGS ROSE INTO AUDIENCE.]*

[SITS. ASSUMES CONFIDENTIAL TONE WITH AUDIENCE.]
I spent most boyhood summers with grandparents on their Wisconsin farm. I once coveted a neighbor's black buck rabbit. I filled my hand with clover and went to the mesh. The awesome buck, munching, dripped saliva on my fingers. The rabbit woman fingered a rusty safety pin holding her apron to her blouse. "Your grandma won't like it." Her eyes were like cold zinc. "Please? I'll pay for him." "No way, Jose."

I gazed between her beefy brows at her third eye where a declivity waited to be smacked with an axe. Seeing that vulnerable spot was almost mystical. You all have one. *[PRESSES HIS FOREHEAD.]* Put your fingers there. Feel it?

"He'll dress out at six or seven pounds," the woman said. "I'm selling him for meat."

I glimpsed her black wooly armpit hair, and smelled the stocking cap pulled over her ears. I reached for the hatchet. "What you doin' with that axe?"

115

I stared into her face.

She banged the hare against a plank. His brain shattered into a host of crabs squirming for shelter. The woman's eyes were the ends of silver screws. I wanted to shove poisoned grapes down her gullet.

She wound a cord around the animal's feet, strung it up on a nail, slit its throat, and hacked off its head. One yank ripped the fur from the body. She did it with the ease she'd have used stripping her kids of a snowsuit.

Without saying goodby, I returned to my grandparents' house. Twilight shadowed my eyes. Behind me, the buck's black fur was glazed. A pair of blackbirds struggled over his guts. I wished I had not dropped the axe. I was not afraid. It was the same back in California. It's the same right here in this room. You don't scare me at all. Do I scare you?

[RISES. GREETS VISITOR.] Oh, here's Rosamund. Come in, sweetheart. Come in! *[TO AUDIENCE]:* Did you hear her scream when she jammed her hand, palm down, in a pool of slime on my dinette table? She **was** angry. I thought she'd spit out her teeth. Her curled hair which was so lovely before she served the veal chops with their little Easter sleeves of butcher paper was a mass of hissing snakes. "I hate life," she said, "and I hate you."

You've all had these domestic, hetero scenes—they lead to splits, divorce, even to murder. Don't deny it. Yes, for a week, during our experiment in living together Ros and I crossed lurid sex lines only when no fat lips sucked us in. It was a four day affair started by her. At the office she lingered near my computer, resting her red nails on the back of my neck. Her cleft chin resembled William Holden's in

"Golden Boy." Now don't laugh. Some women look like men, some men look like women. What's wrong with that? The important thing is to deflect all radiation zapped your way.

[TO ROSAMUND]: Ros, I am neither your lover nor your death's head moth. If you want to play house, cunnilingus, etcetera. [PAUSE.] I'm being creepy? Ros, that's unkind. I've not fucked many women. Sure, I want this to work. I've told you, I usually sleep with men. That doesn't mean I'm gay. No, No. You're threatened. How else can I read your flinging that cheap engagement ring in my face?

[TO AUDIENCE]: We still had two days in our Ensanada motel. She'd demanded no sex until Monday. We'd been watching TV when she suddenly stripped naked. The Mexican evening news was on. "I think about sex all the time," she said, grasping my shaft. Her breasts resembled oval lozenges, not the archetypal balloons of smutty jokes. With a nipple cradled in each hand I had the absurd image of speaking via intercontinental telephone to Prince Charles of England. "I want to suck your big ears," I said.

We rolled to the floor. Ros's buttocks were hairless, and I was pleased, for hairy cracks look best on men. She smoothed my hand along her labia, which I did not mind since we were French kissing. She juiced my index finger, then inserted my penis, riding me and whimpering. A lizard scuttled over my chest. She held me tight, pumping. She bit my throat. She rattled and trembled. When she came, my faked orgasm was true to a picture of the Savior and the Lamb graced with a Palm Sunday leaf. She realized I would not stay, so grandly opened the door for me to leave.

[IS INTROSPECTIVE FOR A MOMENT.] Dear people, I tried. You see, I know what you're thinking: the fact that I've killed homosexuals means I hate myself. If I weren't a coward, I'd kill poor me, and not others. No. That's too simple, folks. Better luck next time.

During my adolescence, at the public library, if a stranger stroked his crotch I feigned disgust, later suffering bad dreams. If a man in cut-offs sat too near on a park bench, I snapped my book shut, threw my half-eaten sandwich to the squirrels, and hurried off. If a "queer" walked his setter on a leash, I moved across the street. Dad always mocked "faggots." So did my classmates even as they masturbated each other in the citrus groves. That's when I preened, kissing Jungian sex shadows flickering on the walls, craving what I despised. And men liked me. I liked being liked, and men galore came onto me. Women almost never made moves. I had tons of sex. Orgies. I stared into sphincters as sweet as freshly split figs. I loved meaty little cock lips. I did not intend to murder.

["PAINT IT BLACK" UP. SINGLE SPOT. KILLER BECKONS TO GUEST WAITING OFF-STAGE.]

Mark, of the white chiselled ass and washboard pecs, I'll try to say I love you, though I may not mean it. A stench of mushrooms, no, of phallic knobs, yes, spewing forth poison where we lie entwined spilling sperm near my massive blue hydrangeas. You don't like the way I'm talking? *[SEEMS TO BE LISTENING.]* You say I've got too much poetry for you? You hate poetry? Moreover, you insulted my luxurious amaryllis, saying their scarlet petals resembled bedraggled rooster tails. How gross.

Mark, you have no body now, or rather you're in bits and pieces, your head in a gas station dumpster, your arms—I've forgotten where I threw them, your torso impaled on a spike. I crave rotting leaves, plums streaming with red flesh, and Korean grass brown with mange. Mark, should I feel more for you than I do? If I could revive you, and fuck you, beautiful boy, I would!

[DISNEY MUSIC.] Folks, Walt's "Magic Kingdom". How many of you have been there? A show of hands, please? Good. I'd have guessed as much. On my last trip, on some great acid I hallucinated mightily. An angel with a red devil's face, wearing a white gown with gossamer wings attached, hovered near the splashy zinnias around the clock tower. [GESTURES.] Look, you can see him now. Damm, he's gone. Security creeps chased him off.

Let's walk up Main Street. If you look to the left, the sidewalk slopes a little. You can see it best if you line up the asses of two lithe men of a similar height. You'll see how one, just for a moment, stands above the other. Those inches are important, for minutiae clue us in to the hidden truths of God.

Disneyland isn't perfect, though it tries to be. Those of you who keep messy cars and houses are intimidated here. You'll never find a stray candy wrapper, a used condom, or a dead opposum. Old people with heart attacks are immediately shuffled out of sight. When an angel flaps his wings to be airborne, you'll hear a plop as though a merganser hit the dirt. Alas, I'm seldom happy here. I try to believe in these cute animals. I try my best to sport a Merry Kingdom Smile. But, I'm numb. That's it: I'm mostly numb.

Let me tell you: I'll never go on the Jungle Cruise again. I don't need the guide's faggot jokes as we approach the black tote-bearers racing up a tree to escape being pronged by a rhino anxious to ram their butt holes. The script writer sure didn't understand sodomy. I wanted to cry.

[LIGHTS DIM. PACES STAGE AS THOUGH LOOKING FOR A VICTIM. MIMES CHOKING ONE TO DEATH.]

It's 3 a.m. The foul deed is done. Kum cooled and hardening, an anal filigree finger-spooled. This chilly night spews sex all over the San Gabriels. I'm shivering. A body in a slime of leaves. A red hibiscus falls, kissing the boys' open lips, concealing his teeth. *[DISCO MUSIC.]*

Hi, surfer, enter. Have a drink. Pills? Your family, you announce, assume you died in LA? Why worry? They probably didn't care much for you, anyway. So, relax. You're safe here. *[PAUSES.]* Yes, you were talking about your life. You'll never be a stock broker, write stories, perm hair, marry, pull teeth, design women's clothes, or sign contracts. Believe me, I know. Why are most of you drop-out, wandering boys so pathetic? If you think of yourselves as shit, how can I possibly love you? *[PAUSES.]* So, we met at 3 a.m., on Coast Highway. Did I come to you? You can write your name, and that's about all? Oh, you can read street signs? Congratulations. Ever heard of William Shakespeare? No, he wasn't a California governor. More pills? *[SARCASTICALLY.]* You're hoping to be "discovered" by a mogul and turned into a sensational TV star?

[LIGHTS ARE NEARLY DARK. TICKING CLOCK. ACTOR STRIPS AND KNEELS OVER THE YOUTH.]

You're on your **left**, your **bad**, side. You'll stay that way, shrivelled salmon-colored scrotum, balls, and all. Good. Your flesh reddens. Rigor mortis is setting in. I fancy crimson peaches, so ripe they attract hordes of wasps. I love you, hustler boy.

[RISES. TO AUDIENCE]: There's been a struggle, for the couch is torn up, my coffee table's upended. And here are

the shoe laces I used to strangle him. *[THROWS THEM OUT INTO AUDIENCE.]* I did try to revive him. I slept for a couple of hours on the floor beside his body. I need some coffee and a shower. *[PAUSE.]* I should have disposed of him hours ago. I'll take him to the San Gabriels. It's only about 5:15. Still dark.

[ACTOR, HOLDING THE CORPSE IN HIS ARMS, FACES THE AUDIENCE.] The pond is almost frozen. The ice shivers like a knife slashing silk. Will I fall through? *[EASES ACROSS THE ICE.]* I'll drop him in. Why doesn't he go under? Has the water inflated his lungs? *[PEERS DOWN.]* His ears are so blue. If I push on his buttocks, he'll drop below the ice sheet. Bubbles stream up. His wretched face kisses the ice from below. His teeth look like a muskrat's. No one has seen us. No one will care.

[LIVING ROOM. SOFT LIGHTS. JUDY GARLAND ON THE STEREO. HE STRIPS TO HIS BRIEFS. A KNOCK ON THE DOOR.] "Who is it?" *[OPENS DOOR.]* I almost forgot. You've turned up. I'm surprised. Sure, sure, you said you would. They all promise to. Public toilet dates aren't too reliable. But, then, you know that, since you're there so much. Well, take off your clothes. Want a drink?

[HE'S NUDE NOW AS HE MOVES TOWARDS AUDIENCE]: This dude, though he has a lithe, white body, sees nothing, yet chatters about everything. Do I like his aerobic shoes? He's washed his socks. He asks why I'm caking his face. My finger under his tongue quivers like a clarinet reed. Warm saliva and panic lather my fingers. *[STRADDLES THE BOY.]* Here, lad, I'll swathe your cock in wet silk. Green highlights the foreskin. Very pretty. Your body's fine-tuned: great tones, from B Major to C minor. Terrific. So, your cock is hard. I'll lick off the slit-tears. Don't die on me, don't fade away! *[SLAPS HIM.]* Hold my balls! Hold my

balls! *[HE ASSAULTS THE BOY WITH COPULATION MOTIONS, SHOUTS IN ORGASM.]*

[IN THE FOLLOWING SPEECH, ALMOST A CHANT, THE ACTOR WORKS TO A CRESCENDO OF FRUSTRATION, AWARE THAT THE MORE BIZARRE HIS KILLINGS THE MORE UNSATISFIED HE REMAINS. HE DELIVERS THIS SPEECH WHILE LYING ON THE FLOOR NEAR HIS VICTIM.]

A car cigarette lighter for scorching eyeballs is not enough. A tree branch with protrusions where limbs were is not enough. I will char both nipples off, and that's not enough. I'll cut off an ear and wrap it around the head of my cock, and I'll kum and that won't be enough. The chopped off nose lying on a Delft plate, one of a set Mom gave me for Christmas, looks like a pig's—and that's not enough. I dance over my beige rug, brush against my crystal in its cherry-wood cupboard, swirl around the corpse, thinking I'm a child blowing chaff from a milkweed pod—and that's not enough. I thrust one hand in the boy's mouth and grab his tongue. My free hand gropes his buttocks, braiding black hairs, yanking them free, rolling them into balls—and this too is not enough. I kiss his lips and eyes—nor is this enough. I sit cross legged. I wad his t-shirt, suck out sweat, suck my own thumb. None of this is enough.

[AT HIS TRIAL. HE WEARS ONLY JOCKEY SHORTS.] Ladies and gentlemen of the jury, spectators, this Court will come to order. Your Honor, you see before you the most notorious killer in U. S. History: 61 men, from ages 13 to 25, Marines, dropouts, dopers. I remember them all. Pictures in my personal album.

[SEES TWO YOUNG WOMEN]: Hi. How are you, ladies? I taught you to run computers. You're still at it, I hope. Was I a good teacher? And you, dear nephew. You brought

your troubles to me, and I helped you with French and math. I was your favorite uncle.

[HE SPOTS A WOMAN, THEN RISES, CHARGED.] Lady, your son was my youngest victim. He was thirteen. You'd kicked him out when he was twelve because you caught him smoking dope. Now you jam your clammy ass in that chair, getting as close to me as you can. Your tears don't fool me. You hated the boy. *[PAUSE.]* Who's that with you? Your old mom? Do you want to give her a heart attack over the grisly visual aids of her butchered grandson? Living color! Better than anything on TV.

Yes, bailiff. Yes, I'll sit back down. My senile parents are here? Please wheel them in.

[WAVES AT HIS FOLKS.] Hi, Mom. Hi, Dad. *[HE KISSES THEIR HEADS.]* How are you, Mom? How's the old Alzheimers? The Press loves my kissing your gray head. Dad, you've shit your pants.

[POSES FOR PICTURE WITH ARM AROUND HIS DAD'S SHOULDER.] Another pose? You journalists, write that my parents' sick eyes flickered when I kissed them. I'm a good son.

[RESUMES HIS SEAT.] The night I was arrested I was dumb, meandering the freeway with a garroted, still warm, Marine, beside me naked in the passenger seat. Unbelievable! Did I want to get caught? My pants were around my ankles. I drove with one hand and had **fun** with the other. "Yes, officer," I said, "This guy was on the road and I'm rushing him to a hospital."

I've three good lawyers, at your, John Q. Public's, expense. And the bailiffs are expensive. One is a WASP going to fat.

The other, a Latino, has thighs like a horse. The prosecuting attorney loves tennis. I want to sleep with him. The judge has a bad vertebra so wears a collar. As for the jury, take a look. Where are my peers? There are only two men among them. My lawyers promise they're not homophobes. Can't tell much about the women, especially the older ones.

[SCANS AUDIENCE.] You men out there, vow you're not homophobes. Can you? See those dead boys up on the screen, boys with scraps of meat stuck to their skeletons, guts, butts, burned eyeballs, and chopped genitals. You'd think they'd scrub these bodies before taking pictures. Look. There's a horrid one—a severed scalp covers his face. Have you ever wondered how the under side of your own scalp looks? Now you know. A rat's heart beats 120 times per minute. I want you to live through this. Right now, at this very moment, take your pulse. I can wait. Of course, you can leave any time you please. Be warned, there's more coming.

They're showing enlarged Polaroids of Robert Christy's corpse found decomposed, jammed into a plastic bag near the El Toro Marine base. *[PAUSES.]* See that green bag? See the oozing body liquor. That lasts for decades, so the forensic people say.

See Christy's tattoos: "Dazed and Confused," "Merlin the Magician," and a puffy red rose. I took these photos in my living room with Christy comatose. This shot you'll love. In case you can't make it out, it's of Christy's anus with a blue-striped sock crammed up it.

[WAVES TO A MIDDLE AGED WOMAN.] Hi, Mrs. Christy. Recognize Robert? When did you last wipe his butt? You see me as Satan, don't you? Your gray anemone eyes, frizzed hair, and that spiral notebook you scribble in don't

fool me. If you could bring Robert back, you'd fling burning silica all over me. Breathe as hard as you can. Being a porker doesn't help, does it? Fat cells don't grieve, only those rich in protein do, and you're obese.

[WAVES AN ARM, SMILING.] My wonderful smile, folks, bugs Mrs. Christy and the other moms. I smile as though I'm in my office eating blackberries, cream, and croissants with morning coffee. I've always had an engaging smile. Do I really look like a killer? Come now.

[WAVES TO A MAN.] Hi there, Pop. I read in the paper that your marriage was lousy. You even divorced your wife. But when they found your son's head off Long Beach Harbor, and his skeleton in manzanita twenty miles down the coast, you got back together with your wife. How do you like identifying your son? Do you like hearing he was a homo? Look at me! Don't turn away. Mothers always glower at me; fathers never do. [SHOUTS]: You dads are cowards! All of you!

[TAKES UP A NOTEBOOK.] You probably wonder what I scribble on these pages. I'd show you, but His Honor won't allow it. I sketch witnesses. I sketch dogs sniffing one another. I draw valentine hearts with arrows shot through them. I draw Santa Clauses with hardons. If I'm found innocent, as I think I'll be, I want to buy some mountain acreage and set up my own cemetery with headstones complete with portrait snapshots for each victim. [PAUSES.] Now, get this. It may be my salvation. My lawyers have engaged a Brain Imaging Professor. He says that as a child I had a brain injury. There's one of my brain "slices" now. It resembles Tia Juana paper flowers, or hot figures in a Turkish carpet. And if you want to be symbolical, in that third slide, there's a snarling leopard's head. The faster the eddies of color, the Imager explains, the more likely it is that those injuries triggered my sexual behavior. Though this judge, alas, is not impressed, a higher court may absolve me. Charles Whitman, the University of Texas Tower murderer, had a large tumor on his right frontal lobe, pressing on his limbic system. They found that out too late though. He had already fried or was hung. I forget which.

[RUBS HIS HEAD AS THOUGH IT ACHES, THEN DONS A PRISON JUMP SUIT AND SITS ON A STOOL, FACING AUDIENCE.] Fog obliterates the full moon. Not very romantic. Well, this jail is not romantic. Even the guard is a downer, fat, with gross lips. Listen. One prisoner's whining and banging a plate. Another is saying his beads. I don't like being so close to Catholic guilt trips. That's not funny, is it? I just didn't want you to see how shitty I feel. They've taken everything except for this toothbrush, soap, underwear, and writing paper. In the morning, so early that the press won't know, they'll drive me to San Quentin. *[MIMES LACING HIS SHOES.]* Might as well get ready, for I don't expect much shut eye tonight. I don't want to die. The appeals could take twenty years. If I were on top of Mt. St. Helen's I wouldn't jump in. I've never been suicidal, though there have been times when I thought I'd explode.

Remember that old artist Piranesi? The Inquisition prisons he fantasized and drew are so peaceful. He keeps you climbing, the stone risers worn by shod feet moving inexoribly to the torture galleries. He loved "the pear," that hollow metal fruit used for killing homosexuals. You inserted it up a rectum, then with a screw twisted it open until the victim screamed and shreds of flesh flew out like jelly fish filaments. A moist sphincter (a rose bud) betrayed you as Uranian, and deserving of such gross metamorphoses. For, as the poet Miklos Radnoti observed: "Little buds / whose noses are always wet don't open / when the sky is filled with whistling." He could have been talking about gorgeous butt holes.

Moreover, these "perverts" always thought they were shards of blue Egyptian tomb glass and by assuming frog postures hoped to hop away. Their whistling priest-tormentors dragged them back and crushed them!

I find Piranesi's drawings sublime. Once I had half a dozen matted, framed, and hung along my bedroom wall, so that immediately on entering they drew you in. Where are they now? All of my possessions are "dispossessed," if you'll excuse the levity, and are in my sister's garage, packed with all else I owned of any value, all towards my being found innocent, on appeal, of these reputed crimes and released.

If I'm gassed, will I float off like a ghost? If I've had nothing will I ever have anything again? What I owned is "sicklied o'er" with slimy maggots and snails, mildew, and the dissolution of wood and paper into dust. You may wrench Pirinasi's images from the man, but never from his brain. I'm on a rack.

[A BELL TOLLS. HE MOVES TO APRON OF STAGE. ALL THE WHILE HE TALKS HE CLINGS TO CELL BARS.] Young friend, sweetheart, my last victim. I've invented a galaxy for you. Fine. Fine. That great moon spatters the sky with light. Magical. You, transcended, are a primary Nova, a bead of radium glowing on the breast of a Nubian prince. I'm sick of tomorrow, and its petty ways—Shakespeare wrote that, didn't he? You quoted one of his sonnets, when I loved you: "How shall I compare thee to a summer's day...." We are tufts of hair and scraps of bone. Railroad spikes on a bed of shaved ice.

[BELL TOLLING CONTINUES. HE NOW FACES AUDIENCE IN FETAL POSITION.] Hairless camels sleep near one

another and near me. Their baby-rat pink cold skins. Ugh! I'm frozen. Tomorrow I'll eat raw pork. *[ON HIS KNEES.]* Young lover, death-angel, don't tell me about tomorrow. "Biplanes are crammed with strawberries," you say. Now that **is** weird. "Rotisseries turn sizzling microscopic suet globules of DNA on spits." That's even crazier. Stop! Stop!

You're rubbing your thumb against your index finger thinking of how I once bit it. Damn. *[STRIKES FLOOR WITH FIST.]* Yes, you are my Nova. But I can blot you out by flashing my eyes. I won't though, for you excite me. Clap your bare ass over my face. I'm your lover. Believe that. Smother me before I am sucked into the horrid mouth of God. God slobbers over there in a corner. See Him? That Dirty Old Man? Park and library boy-diddler. *[RISES.]* He's showing me a path of fire. He's holding a cerecloth. He's lopping off the heads of lizards. He's counting the frigid bodies of sparrows. Will he count the hairs falling from my head? No! No!

[AS STAGE DARKENS, THE FOLLOWING RECITATION BASED ON ITEMS FROM THE LOS ANGELES "TIMES" ARE HEARD OVER THE STEREO SYSTEM, WITH BLEND OF MUSIC HEARD EARLIER ("PAINT IT BLACK" and "LULLABY"). THE VOICE RECITING BECOMES INCREASINGLY INAUDIBLE. MUSIC OUT.]

Prosecutors maintain that a paper found in the murderer's car trunk at the time of his arrest on May 14, 1983, is a death list, with entries dating back to late 1971.

STABLE. Wayne Joseph Dukette, 30, of Long Beach, found dead at bottom of a ravine in Orange County. Suffered from alcohol intoxication. Last seen in Stables Bar, Sunset Beach.
ANGEL. Unsolved.

EDM. Edward Daniel Moore, 20, a Marine from Camp Pendelton, found Dec. 26, 1972. Found at a freeway interchange. Strangled three days earlier. Sock stuffed up anus.

HARI KARI. Unsolved.

AIRPLANE HILL. A "John Doe" found on Airplane Hill in Huntington Beach. Sodomized and emasculated.

TWIGGIE. James Dale Reeves, 19, of Cypress Calif., found near freeway in S. Orange County. Nude except for T-shirt. 4' tree branch shoved up his anus.

VINCE M. Vincent Cruz Mestas, 23, of Long Beach, found at bottom of ravine in San Bernardino mountains. Shoeless. Sock stuffed into anus. Genitals mutilated. Hands severed from body. Strangulated.

SKATES. John William Leras, 17, of Long Beach, found Jan. 4, 1975, floating in surf at Sunset Beach. Wooden surveyor's stake stuffed up anus. Was seen the day before boarding a bus en route to a roller skating rink carrying new skates. Suffocated.

PARKING LOT. Keith David Crotwell, 19, of Long Beach. Severed head found near a jetty. Skeletal remains, lacking hands, found that October near the El Toro Marine base in S. Orange County.

DEODORANT. Robert Avila, 16, of Los Angeles, found July 29, 1982 near Hollywood Freeway. Known as heavy deodorant user. Strangled.

DOG. Raymond Davis, 13, found July 29, 1982, next to body of Robert Avila, #20. He was visiting relatives in LA and had gone to a park to seek his lost dog. Strangled.

HAWTH OFF HEAD. "John Doe," found April 22, 1973. Torso on Wilmington. Right leg on Terminal Island Freeway, Long Beach. Head at 7th St. and Redondo in Long Beach. Left leg found behind Broom Hilda's bar in Sunset Beach. Strangled. Emasculated.

JOHN DOE. No. 299, found Aug. 29, 1979, in a dumpster behind at Union 76 Station in Long Beach. Arms severed at the shoulders, legs at hip joints. Head severed. Only head, left leg, and torso recovered. Sock in body cavity.

NEW YEAR'S EVE. Mark Howard Hall, 22, of Santa Ana, Calif., found Jan. 3, 1976, Santiago Canyon. Eyes and genitals mutilated with an automobile cigarette lighter. Emasculated.

PORTLAND DENVER. Michael Shawn O'Fallon, 17, found July 17, 1980, near Interstate 5, Salem. Nude. Sodomized. Strangled.

PORTLAND BLOOD. Michael Duane Cluck, 18, found April 10, 1981, near Interstate 5, Goshen, Oregon. Sodomized. Bludgeoned 31 times on back of head.

GR 2. Dennis Patrick Alt and Christopher Alan Schoenborn, two cousins, both found together Dec. 9, 1982, in field near Grand Rapids, Michigan. Asphyxiated by choking. Schoenborn found nude with Amway pen stuffed up anus. Strangled. A bottle opener belong to one of the victims and Schoenborn's jacket were later found.

DART 405. Michael Joseph Inderbieten, 20, of Long Beach, found Nov. 18, 1978, at freeways interchange. Nude, except for pants pulled down below his waist. Emasculated and sodomized. Suffocated.

OTHER BOOKS BY ROBERT PETERS
CAN BE ORDERED DIRECTLY
(Most are Out Of Print)

THE POET AS ICE-SKATER _____

Anthology of poems to Whitman, Lorca, Ginsberg, Jack Spicer, Goethe, and Arthur Rimbaud. Out of print.

Manroot Books, 1976.   Paper $10.00

GAUGUIN'S CHAIR: NEW AND SELECTED POEMS _____

Selection of poems, including the poet's much-praised elegy, *Songs For A Son*, and a seminal interview. Out of print.

Crossing Press, 1977. 0-912278-74-9   Paper $10.00

THE DROWNED MAN TO THE FISH _____

Poems commemorating marriage breakup and moving to a gay life.

New Rivers, 1978. 0-898230-02-0   Paper $7.00

WHAT JOHN DILLINGER MEANT TO ME _____

Poems about the maturing gay psyche on the Wisconsin farm. Out of print.

Sea Horse Press, 1983. 0-933322-09-7   Paper $10.00

MAD LUDWIG OF BAVARIA: POEMS AND A PLAY _____

Much-heralded poetic treatment of the life of a homosexual king. Out of print.

Cherry Valley Eds., 1984. 0-916156-82-6   Paper $7.00

HAWKER _____

Verse biography of the very eccentric vicar, mystic, and poet, Stephen Hawker. Out of print.

Unicorn Press, 1985. 0-87775-165-X   Cloth $20.00
                     0-87775-166-8   Paper $10.00

KANE _____

Verse portrait of Elisha Kent Kane; men struggling for survival in the Arctic wastes. Out of print.

Unicorn Press, 1986. 0-87775-468-4   Cloth $20.00
                     0-87775-169-8   Paper $10.00

THE BLOOD COUNTESS: POEMS AND A PLAY
Story of the notorious 17th century lesbian mass murderer. Out of print.

Cherry Valley, 1987. 0-916156-80-X   Cloth $15.00
    0-916156-81-8   Paper $9.00

SHAKER LIGHT
Poems about the Shaker experience in America under the mystic Ann Lee. Out of print.

Unicorn Press, 1988. 0-87775-200-1   Cloth $20.00
    0-87775-201-X   Paper $10.00

CRUNCHING GRAVEL: ON GROWING UP IN THE THIRTIES
Memoir of life in rural poverty and of the author's homosexual stirrings. Out of print.

Mercury House, 1988. 0-916515-34-6   Cloth $20.00

HAYDON
Poems about the struggles for recognition and the suicide of the famous Victorian painter and author. Out of print.

Unicorn Press, 1989. 0-87775-219-2   Cloth $20.00
    0-87775-220-6   Paper $10.00

GOOD NIGHT, PAUL
Intimate and memorable poems by and to a gay lover on their twenty-year anniversary.

GLB Publishers, 1991   1-879194-06-6   Paper $8.95

(We pay the sales tax.)

Book Sub-Total US $ _____

Add $2.00 per book for shipping US $ _____
($4.00 for overseas)   **TOTAL US $**

Send check or money order (no credit cards or phone orders, please) to:

GLB Publishers
P.O. Box 78212, San Francisco, CA 94107